D1046647

THE GOLDEN CALVES

Also by Louis Auchincloss

FICTION

The Indifferent Children
The Injustice Collectors
Sybil
A Law for the Lion
The Romantic Egoists
The Great World and Timothy Colt
Venus in Sparta
Pursuit of the Prodigal
The House of Five Talents
Portrait in Brownstone
Powers of Attorney
The Rector of Justin
The Embezzler
Tales of Manhattan
A World of Profit
Second Chance
I Come as a Thief
The Partners
The Winthrop Covenant
The Dark Lady
The Country Cousin
The House of the Prophet
The Cat and the King
Watchfires
Narcissa and Other Fables
Exit Lady Masham
The Book Class
Honorable Men
Dairy of a Yuppie
Skinny Island

NONFICTION

Reflections of a Jacobite
Pioneers and Caretakers
Motiveless Malignity
Edith Wharton
Richelieu
A Writer's Capital
Reading Henry James
Life, Law and Letters
Persons of Consequence: Queen Victoria
and Her Circle
False Dawn: Women in the
Age of the Sun King

THE GOLDEN CALVES

LOUIS AUCHINCLOSS

1988

Houghton Mifflin Company

BOSTON

Library of Congress Cataloging-in-Publication Data

Auchincloss, Louis.
The golden calves / Louis Auchincloss.
p. cm.
ISBN 0-395-47691-7
I. Title.
PS3501.U25G6 1988
813'.54—dc 19 87-32178
CIP

Printed in the United States of America

P 10 9 8 7 6 5 4 3 2 1

In Loving Memory
of

DOROTHY TUER

for twenty years my
indispensable amanuensis

THE GOLDEN CALVES

1

ANITA VOGEL'S office in the Museum of North America, like those of the other curators in the porticoed marble edifice on Central Park West, seemed designed to make its occupant feel that she was usurping the space of a more important functionary. The ceiling was too high, the window that overlooked a verdant park too big, the door too richly paneled and the knob, shaped like a mountain goat's curly horns, too shiny for one who supervised only that section of the decorative arts department represented by the collection of Miss Evelyn Speddon. Some justification might have been found in the reflection that such disparity between appearance and reality was true of the institution itself, whose splendid columns and awesome façade hardly reflected the precarious state of its exchequer. Constructed in 1930 by a banker who had subsequently lost the fortune with which he had intended to endow it, the museum had in the ensuing four and a half decades suffered a career of constant crises relieved only by desperate fund-raising campaigns. By 1975, however, even one so naturally pessimistic as Anita could indulge the hope that with a bright new acting director and a forward-looking chairman of the board, the museum's "image" — to use the term sacred to public relations — was brightening.

Miss Speddon, whose vast eclectic collection of Americana, from pre-Columbian figurines to chaste Shaker rockers, was in constant process of transmittal to the museum, had personally decorated Anita's office, adorning it in the protective apparel of the art patroness and shielding it from the jealous eye of the administration. The rushing steam engines, the galloping horses and gliding schooners of Currier & Ives covered the walls; a multicolored Tiffany lamp illuminated the desk; the shouting reds of a Pueblo carpet pranced on the floor. "I like to feel at home when I come here," the old lady had retorted to Anita's feebly voiced protest. "You say that all these beautiful things set you apart from the other curators. Well, that's just what I want. Your office is my embassy in what I sometimes regard as almost enemy territory."

A collector and her institutional beneficiary, Miss Speddon meant, had always to be to some extent at loggerheads. As her field covered North America in all phases of its history, she had been almost obliged to come to terms with a museum dedicated to that continent, and she had hoped, by conveying a portion of her things in her lifetime, to be able to supervise their exhibition, and, by taking over Anita's full time and salary, to build an outpost in the museum's field of policy-making that would survive her.

But Miss Speddon, Anita feared, was getting too old and parting with her things too slowly to be able to accomplish her grand scheme before the end. It was becoming more and more difficult for her to surrender her beloved artifacts, each of which was a kind of baby to her, and Anita was reluctant to hurry the process, suspecting that Miss Speddon's very heartbeats might depend on the proximity of her collection and that for her to give it all up might tie the final passage of title to the final one of life. Nor could she visualize what her own life would be without the patroness who had provided her with the only home and love she had known.

"I should be like the Assyrian bas-reliefs in her front hall," Anita murmured to herself. "Not a part of the American collection. Not really a part of anything once the person who cares is gone."

The Assyrian warriors, with their high helmets, eagle beaks and cruel profiles, had been bought by Miss Speddon's father and, although outside his daughter's chosen field, had been loyally retained by her after his death. Anita, passing them in the hall every morning as she went to work, viewed them with affection and fancied that she could sense a corresponding reaction in the way their grip on their spears seemed to relax, like the slackening bodies of German shepherds recognizing a friendly presence.

"I never really lived before Miss Speddon took me in. How shall I live afterwards?"

But she knew Miss Speddon did not like her to be moody. Miss Speddon always insisted that she was not only young but pretty. Anita knew that she was not really that, yet she had a few cherished illusions. She liked to imagine that her brooding gaze lent an aura of sensitivity and intelligence to a face that might have else appeared merely long and pale. In the same way she hoped that her quick step and straight carriage gave grace to a figure which might without them have seemed to verge on the gaunt. It was a favorite fantasy of hers that when she pulled back the long dark hair that sometimes fell across her forehead, people who might at first have thought of Anita Vogel as a bit dry, a bit on the plain side, with a touch of the old maid or at least the bluestocking, would now perceive that, no, she was really something rarer, something almost fine, a presence not for the usual taste but for the discerning eye. And yet always, even at her present age of thirty-two (and almost thirty-three at that), she would blush at such absurdities, shake her head impatiently and turn back to whatever was on her desk.

And now she did so, only to be interrupted by the unceremonious opening of her door without a knock.

"I thought I'd catch you at the crossword! I was wrong. You're not even doing that."

"Fire me."

"If I only dared!" The acting director was constantly cheerful. "But what would the great Miss Speddon say? Anyway, I've come to see the model of the colonial kitchen."

Mark Addams exuded more self-confidence than even an acting director aiming at the permanent post need exude. Everything about him seemed designed to promote a sense in the observer of a fresh broom sweeping clean, or a new and sparkling wine in an old bottle. He was on the short side but trimly and tightly put together; he had curly blond hair and a bright, fresh, clean boyish face that did not go with his age of thirty-five except when a flush of anxiety betrayed that he was trying not to look quite so pleased with himself. Oh, he could do the job, he seemed to be telling you; he could turn the museum around, he could drag it into the twenty-first century, if need be, but were people really going to understand how good he was? Mark had come to the museum from a public relations firm. He had to know that every scholar on the staff was praying to see the glitter in those friendly gray-green eyes extinguished.

"You're psychic," she admitted. "The drawings just came in." She pointed to the table on which was spread out the blueprint of a diorama of a kitchen in Peter Stuyvesant's New Amsterdam.

"Perhaps not so psychic as you suppose," Mark retorted, going over to study it. "If we poor directors relied on being informed!" There followed two minutes of silent contemplation. "Well, I suppose it will do for a start. But I confess I look forward to the day when the gallery of Speddon period rooms reaches an era of greater elegance. In Williamsburg, doesn't your heart leap when you get away from all those pots and pans and tinkers' shops to the glory of the governor's palace?"

"I never heard anything so snobbish! That's just what was wrong with the way we used to be taught history. All that emphasis on the rich and mighty. On palaces and battles. What's wrong with a tinker's shop?"

But Mark was not in the least abashed. "Why should a museum be concerned with the lowly? With grubby pictures of drab lives? I think history in a museum should be a statement of its greatest themes. With portraits and busts and crowns and scepters and all the finest jewelry and décor!"

"You should have been director at Versailles."

"We have plenty of it right here in New York. With English governors and old manors and silver. Not to mention the Astors and Vanderbilts."

"Is this the Museum of North America or the Museum of Tiffany and Company?"

He laughed his high, braying laugh. It was a laugh that seemed to annihilate criticism. "That's right, Anita. Keep me in my place. Be the gloomy Gus who stood behind the Roman general in his triumph, muttering, 'Remember: you're only dust.' If they ever set up that museum for the Holocaust, you might be just the curator they need."

Anita's hands flew to her cheeks in horror. "Oh, never, never! Never that." On a dank cold dawn she was in a stockade with a fence of barbed wire rising above the dripping black walls. She shook her head. Mark was staring at her. Why did it have to be so vivid to her? Was it not presumptuous to seem to share agonies to which she had never been exposed? Or *had* she been, in a former life? Or *would* she be, in a future one? People couldn't go through such horrors and have others immune. It could not be!

"What's wrong, Anita? Have I upset you?"

"What a horrible idea for a museum!"

Why didn't he go away? She had a place for Mark in her fantasies, a private place where they even did disgusting things together. Oh, God, if he could ever read her mind! But it was all right, wasn't it, to have fantasies if no one suspected them? Still, it was upsetting when he was right there in front of her, being absurdly kind to her, being absurdly charming, damn him. And of course not caring for her any more than he cared for his old grandmother, if he had one.

"You're right," she continued breathlessly. "Museums should be filled with beautiful things. I agree with that. But even simple things in a New Amsterdam kitchen can be beautiful."

"I was only kidding you."

Anita picked up her buzzing telephone and heard a woman's voice. "Is the director with you, Miss Vogel? Will you ask him to call Mr. Claverack?" But even when she had delivered the message, he did not leave her to call the chairman of the board. With an ostentatious show of independence, he turned to the window and gazed over the park.

"You know, Anita, if I do become director, I'm going to need friends in this joint."

She shivered. How could he go on this way! "Of course you're going to be director. Everyone knows the search committee is only a formality. Mr. Claverack has made his choice, and what's more, he's made the right one."

"Thanks. But one never knows with Sidney Claverack. At his most cordial he may have already turned against you. And this place is full of people who would be only too happy to slit my throat. That's always the difference between profit and non-profit institutions. In a business everyone binds up the boss when he starts bleeding. Even if they hate his guts, they know their income depends on him. But in a museum or a school the first red drop sends the sharks into a frenzy. They take for granted the endowment will still pay their salaries after they've devoured him."

"You make us sound so awful."

"I make us sound the way we are. That's why I'm going to need people like you to help me keep a level head. The pressures in this place are unbelievable. I've had to make each of the major trustees feel that he has me in his pocket. And each one expects me to be a different kind of director."

Anita thought of the other great collector on the board. "What kind does Mr. Hewlett want you to be?"

"Peter Hewlett expects me to keep his collection intact in a separate gallery if it comes to the museum."

"But that's against Mr. Claverack's policy! If every donor did that, you'd have fifty museums, not one."

"If the collection's great enough, don't you have to compromise?"

"No! The museum should stand together on that. Every artifact should be in its correct historical place, not all huddled together promiscuously."

Mark smiled at her vehemence. "What about your sacred Miss Speddon?"

"Miss Speddon attaches no conditions to her gifts except that they be permanently shown."

"Still, a permanent showing . . . that's a fairly stiff condition."

"You don't have to take them if you don't want to show them."

"Even if they turn out to be fakes?"

"Miss Speddon doesn't buy fakes."

"All right, all right!" He threw up his hands in surrender. "We'll let that pass. Though I think you may find that your great patroness is not quite so rigid as you suppose. Anyway, promise me that you'll be my friend. My best friend. If I'm named director."

Really, the man was unbearable. How could he torture her

so? Only by closing her eyes could she bring herself to ask what she now asked. "What will Miss Norton say to that?"

Chessie Norton was the female lawyer with whom Mark had been having an affair for the past three years. The only reason they didn't share an apartment was that Mark feared it might hurt him with some of the older trustees, and in particular with Miss Speddon.

"Chessie perfectly understands that my life in the museum is as much a thing apart from her as her law firm is apart from me. Chessie would not dream of taking offense at any of my professional relationships."

For once Anita found the looming presence of Carol Sweeters in her doorway a relief. Mark, nodding to him only curtly, at once took his leave.

"Well, well, *well!* We seem to be great favorites of Young Lochinvar these days. He'll be sweeping you off on his charger down Central Park West. And those of us who are so unblessed as to form a less agreeable image on the lordly pupil of his hawklike eye must learn to cling to the fringes of your privileged skirt."

Carol Sweeters had a way of staring at a person from a doorway as if that individual's appearance had aroused in him the same boredom and disgust that his own was apt to evoke, returning to the world with interest its presumed reaction to himself. It was not so much that he was plain as that he seemed somehow unfinished, or even slept in. His sandy hair was messy; his features were bunched together in the center of a rotund countenance; his figure, which might have been tolerable if better distributed, tended to bulge and tighten in the wrong places. And yet he held one's attention. He was intelligent, damnably intelligent, and his character had the strength of perpetual aggressiveness.

"What do you want, Carol?"

"Want!" His eyebrows soared in outrage. "Oh, I see. We

cannot obtrude, can we, on the sacred time of the eminence not so *grise* of the new administration? Well, if I may crave a word with one who was not always so averse to the approaches of your humble servant, who even, if I presume to recall it, permitted, on one or more occasions, her chaste lips to be — shall we say brushed? — by the coarser ones of . . ."

"Oh, Carol, shut up! You're disgusting."

"Disgusting *now*. But less disgusting once upon a time."

"Get on with it, please. Whatever it was you came in for."

"I shall be brief." But the mottled color of his cheeks belied the coolness of his tone. She knew he was furious. "Have you heard what Lochinvar . . . ?"

"Let us call him by his right name."

"What Addams — excuse me, *Mr.* Addams — plans to do with the little music hall on the third floor?"

"No. But what concern is that of mine?"

"A straw in the wind, my dear. No more. But enough of them may forecast the storm that will blow little me away — and thee, too, I trow — and maybe even the great Miss Speddon herself, with all her cloud-topped towers and gorgeous palaces — yea, leaving not a rack behind!"

"Must you be so dramatic?"

"It gives me a touch of dignity when, like Cassandra, I am sure not to be believed. But to the point. If you were not so infatuated with our boss-to-be, you would roundly condemn his proposal to remove the manuscripts of early American music to the gloomy Gehenna of the library vault and put in their place some tawdry prints of opera sets. Instead of a unique collection of American colonial work we shall be faced with silly scenes from such overflogged European dead horses as *Aïda* and *Il Trovatore*."

"That show is designed to illustrate the evolution of American operatic production. Isn't that indigenous? Isn't it educational?"

"Ah, educational! The holy word. You'd think we had no

more schools or colleges. I thought museums were for the *educated*. For persons of taste and cultivation. Not for chattering schoolchildren pinching one another's fannies while some dreary docent drones on about the influence of this on that."

"Really, Carol, you're a hopeless elitist."

"Art is elitist. Beauty is elitist!"

"And the public be damned."

"The public be double-damned! I can remember a day when you weren't so far from my persuasion. When an idealistic young woman was happy to lose herself in the study of an ancient civilization and think nothing of museum shops full of vulgar dolls and costume jewelry or of planning shows of everything but the artifacts in one's own institution. But that was before we fell under the spell of Young Lochinvar."

She always had the hateful feeling that Carol could read her mind. For how else could he deduce her emotional concern with Mark from the latter's occasionally dropping into her office, a courtesy he rendered to all the curators? Carol was a kind of fiend. Had she not felt his power over herself? She detested being alone with him, even in her own office with the door wide open.

"I haven't changed that much," she said sullenly.

"Only in that you have become the slave of fashion. I suppose you shouldn't be too much censured for that. Fashion rules our world, from antinuclear protests to the size of bikinis. But beware! Fashion can be a merciless tyrant. It can become the storm of which I just warned you."

"What on earth are you talking about?"

He raised a solemn finger as he paused for effect. "I am predicting, Anita Vogel, that within a century of Evelyn Speddon's demise her collection will have been scattered over the auction markets of this nation from sea to shining sea!"

"And why do you assume such a horrible thing?"

"Because your dear lady has collected everything there is to collect. With the inevitable result that in each succeeding decade at least one tenth of her artifacts will be out of fashion. And things out of fashion are necessarily disposed of."

"Aren't you forgetting the little matter of her will?"

"I forget neither her will nor the firm that is drawing it. Is it not Claverack's? But even if she puts in a hundred restrictive clauses, a judge in equity, interpreting the dead mind as it would have functioned had it existed at the moment of decision — i.e., as does his honor's — will provide a key to open every lock. That is what the enlightened law professor of our day calls the nature of the judicial process."

"I don't believe you!"

"Meaning you won't. And anyway, you needn't. You won't live to see it all. As I say, it will take a hundred years."

"Oh, go away, please, Carol, go away. You just love to torture me."

Desperate, she covered her eyes with her hands. When she looked up, to her surprise and relief he was gone. It still lacked fifteen minutes to closing time, but she decided to go home, as she had at last learned to call Miss Speddon's mansion on East 36th Street, lonely survivor of an era when Murray Hill had been fashionable. If Anita's life at times struck her as a scuttling through dark alleys to blessed havens, this dwelling was certainly the greatest of the latter, far safer than the museum itself, for there were no acting directors, no Carol Sweeterses there, only the friendly ancient Irish maids, moving silently through dim, cool chambers to administer to the perfect comfort of a wonderful old lady surrounded by objects of incomparable beauty.

Emerging from the taxi that she had extravagantly taken, Anita paused to gaze gratefully up at the welcoming façade whose heavily rusticated ground floor seemed almost too hefty for the support of the second and third stories of red limestone and the green mansard roof popping with bull's-eye windows.

Then, taking her key, she let herself into the front hall to greet the Assyrian warriors with a silently breathed assurance that she would do her best to protect them from a threatened power of even greater evil than their cruel profiles seemed to evoke.

She found Miss Speddon alone in the parlor, sitting in her usual upright position in the middle of a high-backed divan before a silver tea service that might have meant, to one unfamiliar with her ways, that she was expecting a dozen guests.

"Why how nice, dear, that you're home early, just in time for a cup of tea. And to think I was just feeling the least bit sorry for myself at being all alone."

Miss Speddon was a tall, thin, bony woman who dressed in lively colors, often red, but she wore no make-up, scorning to compromise with time's ravages, professing on the contrary to welcome them, in accordance with her stoutly maintained theory that each minute of life was as good, or should be, as any other. Her strong, oval, slightly equine face was framed by long hair of snowy white, parted in the middle of her scalp, and her unadorned neck and ears gave emphasis to the big-stoned rings that turned around on her long thin fingers.

"I had a visitor this morning," she observed after she had filled Anita's cup. "None other than your young acting director."

"Oh? He didn't tell me."

"Does he tell you everything?" Was Miss Speddon being arch?

"Not at all. But associating me, as he does, so entirely with you, I should have thought he might mention it when he was in my office this afternoon."

"Does he come often to your office?"

Anita wondered in dismay whether the whole world was going mad. "Dear Miss Speddon, what in the world are you driving at?"

"Simply that he strikes me as having a more than casual interest in you."

"He certainly has a more than casual interest in *you*. And in your collection. As I suppose he should have. And certainly a more than casual interest in the fund with which he hopes to see it endowed."

"Dear me, how mercenary the world must seem to you! But that brings me exactly to the point I've been for some time wanting to make. That I may have been remiss in introducing you to that world. How many years have you been living with me, dear?"

"Three years and three months."

"How precisely you know it!"

"It shows that, contrary to the belief of many theologians, there *can* be time in heaven."

Miss Speddon's little smile acknowledged the too florid compliment. "Dear child, how gracefully you put it. But in all that time how often have you entertained your friends here?"

"You had all my family here for my thirtieth birthday. A good dozen in all, counting all the halfs and steps."

"But *friends*, Anita. When have we had your friends?"

Anita sighed at having to go into this again. For Miss Speddon was constantly offering her the chance for hospitality. It was simply that Miss Speddon forgot. "You've offered to ask my friends here again and again. Nobody could have been more profusely generous. It is I who have been the reluctant one."

"Maybe I shouldn't have paid attention to your reluctance."

"Maybe I haven't any friends."

"And maybe that is something I should have remedied," the older woman insisted. "And given some dinner parties for young people. Well, it's never too late to start. Let's have a party and ask Mr. Addams."

Anita could hardly suppress a little groan. "Dear, *dear* Miss Speddon, won't you ever realize that I'm perfectly happy the way things are? That I have adored being included in your life and taken in by your friends? That I want nothing else? Can't we just go on as we have been?"

But Miss Speddon could be inexorable where she spied a duty

she might have shirked. "Certainly not. I must consider your best interests. I stand to some degree *in loco parentis*."

"Oh, altogether! I have no family now but you."

Miss Speddon frowned. "You must not say that or even think it. Remember your mother and father."

"But they're not my mother and father! You know that. They adopted me only because they thought they couldn't have children, and when they did, my sole use was gone. Oh, I'm not saying they haven't been decent enough; they have, and so have my stepmother and both my stepfathers and all the halfs and steps, but they don't any of them really care about me, and they were tickled pink when you took me over and all my problems. Why can't I adopt somebody, too? I adopt you as my mother!" Then she thought of Miss Speddon's fortune and blushed very red. "Oh, of course, I don't mean anything legal or having to do with rights or anything like that! I mean just here at home. Oh, Miss Speddon, what must you think of me!"

"I think of you as a very dear young woman whom I regard as a kind of ward. I don't in the least mind being entirely frank about legal matters. I shall not leave you any substantial part of my estate —"

"Oh, Miss Speddon, please!" Anita cried in agony. What kind of a mad day was she having?

"Let me finish, dear. I was raised with very strict principles about inherited money. I believe it is incumbent upon me to leave the bulk of the Speddon money that my grandfather made to his descendants, except to the extent that I may deflect it to charity. Accordingly, I am leaving my collection and two thirds of my Speddon estate to the museum, and one-third to my nephew and niece. As the latter are very well off, this should satisfy them. But I also have the money that I call 'my own,' the much more modest estate that my mother left me. *She* had no other descendants, so with this I may provide for friends and servants, including you, my dear. It is no fortune that I'll be leaving you, but it should keep you decently, and I shall request the museum to retain you to look after my things."

Anita burst into tears. "I don't want to live after you!"

"But you will, my dear, and I trust you'll have a long and happy life. And as you choose to regard me as a mother, I think you should heed my advice. Which is this: do not rule out the idea of marriage. Keep an open mind. If the right man comes along —"

Anita could bear it no longer. "If you mean Mark Addams, I think you should know he has no thoughts of me in that line. He has a long-standing affair with a lawyer in Mr. Claverack's firm."

"A lawyer?" Miss Speddon's lips were pursed to a small *o* of surprise and distaste.

"I think you've actually met her."

"Oh, a woman. For a moment I thought you meant . . . We have to be ready for anything these days. But these liaisons must be expected of young men. They don't last forever."

"But this one seems quite permanent. They'll probably get married. And even if they don't, I have no interest like that in Mark. Let us not talk about him, please. And I promise you that I'll keep an open mind about marriage. There! Will that do? Now, why don't you tell me what you and the acting director discussed? If it was not private, that is. For I'm sure he didn't come here to tell you how much he admired me."

"No, that was just my inference. He came, at my suggestion, to discuss my will. I gave him a copy of it and asked him for his suggestions."

"Which, knowing Mark, I'm sure he had."

"Yes, and actually some rather interesting ones. He thinks I should leave more questions to the discretion of the museum than I have."

"What, for example?"

"Well, whether a particular object should be kept or sold."

"Sold?"

"Don't look so horrified, dear. It's not that they'd do it. But as he explained, we are confronted these days with the cleverest art forgeries. It would be absurd if a museum were obliged to continue to display a Healy or an Eastman Johnson after it was established it had been painted by some smart fraud in an attic in Brooklyn."

"If he were that smart, maybe he's a better painter than Healy or Johnson."

But to Miss Speddon, as to all collectors, the art forger was the arch-heretic, worthy of being burned alive. "And then there is the question of new valuations. The museum should be free to move things about to give prominence to artifacts coming into or going out of fashion. Mr. Addams cited Mrs. Gardner's museum in Boston as a case in point, where the administration can't even rehang a picture. The dead hand, he said, has frozen the whole collection."

"Oh, Miss Speddon, I beg of you, don't listen to him!"

Anita had jumped to her feet. She was trembling so that even Miss Speddon's old eyes could take it in.

"I'm afraid, my dear, that you're overwrought. Perhaps our talk today has been a bit too personal for you. Why don't you go upstairs and have a nice hot bath, and then we'll have an early supper and listen to my new recording of the Mahler Fifth?"

2

ANITA'S sense of having been as much a stranger in the family nest as an oversized cuckoo fledgling hatched from an egg covertly deposited by a slovenly mother in the home of neat, orderly bluebirds was more justified by the facts than are many such feelings of alienation. Her adoptive father was a bright, energetic advertising man; her mother, a competent fashion designer. They had been married for three years without issue and had decided to adopt a baby girl just before Sam Vogel was sent overseas in the war. But when he returned they proceeded to have two babies of their own, to divorce and remarry, and, amid all the proliferation of offspring of different matches, and of homes in Manhattan, East Orange and Rye, the thin, dark-haired, introspective and rather gangling oldest child had always been conscious of an air of faint surprise whenever she turned up.

It was not that they weren't nice to her. They were. But there was a resounding normalcy about them all, a blare of loud laughter, a constant whirring of balls being thrown and caught, from which she tended to shrink to an all-too-easily forgotten isolation. She had performed her function, after all. The fact of her adoption, as so often happens, had rendered the adopters not only fertile but fecund. She had been a device that, had she not been human, would have been disposed of. And then, too, the advertising father and designing mother had only moderately prospered; they had done well enough by normal standards, but their broods were large, and the private education deemed mandatory in the metropolitan area took more than all the income there was. Oh, true, Anita was paid for as well; she was by no means Cinderella with the wicked sisters, but she would never have presumed to ask for the extra tuition for a master of art history degree on top of her bachelor's from Hunter. For that she had paid with a hard-won partial scholarship, her wages as a night waitress and an occasional check from her mother; and when, with the aid of a professor who had taken a particular interest in her work, she had secured a job at the Museum of North America, there seemed to be a feeling among all the Vogels, understandably enough, that she should be henceforth pretty much on her own. She would of course continue to go to her father's in East Orange on Thanksgiving and to her mother's in Rye for Christmas, and there would always be occasional summer weekends, and much would be made of her on each arrival — for half an hour. It was all right; Anita neither expected nor really wanted anything more. She liked her room on top of a brownstone only two blocks from where she worked. The museum had soon become her family and her life.

She worked for three years in the pre-Columbian department, which embraced the vast field from the early Mayas to the Esquimaux and whose overall head was Carol Sweeters. She did not at first work directly for him, as she was assigned to a subdepartment of East Coast Indians in which he took little interest, but when he was putting together a major show of the museum's Yucatán artifacts, and the assistant in charge suddenly left for a job in another museum, he selected Anita, quite arbitrarily as she then thought, to take the defector's place. But she soon discovered he had been watching her more closely than she had supposed.

"I note that you have been faithful over a few things, Miss Vogel," he told her in his sneering tone. "I shall now make you lord over many."

"But may I go back to my Seminoles when we've done the show?"

"If you still wish it then. You have been working with savages. The Mayas, you will find, had a civilization in some ways as high as our own. Not that that's saying much."

"Because they studied the stars and devised a calendar?"

"And because they built beautiful temples and adorned them with beautiful objects. I miss my guess, Miss Vogel, if you do not lose your heart to the Mayas."

Anita dutifully took home several books on the Mayas and read them at night. She became fascinated by their concept of an agrarian society that kept warfare to a minimum. Indeed, they had appeared to regard it only as a defensive measure against invading tribes. When left to themselves, it seemed, they enjoyed a tranquil existence under clear blue skies, worshiping their strange gods on the high steps of their wonderful temples. There was, it was true, some suggestion in the books of human sacrifice, but Anita eagerly pursued the evidence that this aspect of their ritual may have been exaggerated or misunderstood by earlier historians. She had all her life suffered from a violent horror of all forms of bloodshed, with terrible nightmares about people being tortured or burned alive or devoured by tawny beasts. Indeed, she had often been afraid to go to bed at all, a state of affairs that had done little to contribute to her popularity in those early homes of dreamless sleepers.

Carol Sweeters was then in his late thirties, unmarried, and, despite his ugliness, had a reputation of success with the ladies at the museum. Anita was never sure how much she really liked him, but she could not help being intrigued by all that he took for granted, including his bland assumption that she could ask for nothing better than to share his bed.

"What are you holding out for?" he demanded one night in a cafeteria — he was notoriously stingy on dates — when she for the second time firmly declined to go back to his apartment. "A proposal of marriage? Don't you think I could do better?"

"Much. And so could I."

"Oh, I see your game. You think you're the shy, intense type that's going to catch the millionaire sated with silly society beauties. Jane Eyre and Mr. Rochester. Or that girl in *Rebecca* with Max de Winter. Except you're not apt to find Rochester or de Winter in the Indian department of a second-class museum on Central Park West. Or do you dream of a passing trustee? 'And what is *your* name, my pretty little assistant curator?' Dream on, poor girl!"

"Well, if I do catch one, I'll promise to make him raise your salary. So you can afford to take the underlings you plan to seduce to better places for dinner."

He cackled with pleasure. "So that's it! Here I've been wasting my time talking about ancient tribes, and all the while you could be had for some crêpe suzettes and a bottle of bubbly."

"You might try them, anyway."

"But I will! Shall we adjourn to some high-cost nightery? Before going to my apartment?"

"I'm not going to your apartment, Carol. Please understand that."

"You find me so unattractive?"

"I don't sleep with every man I find not unattractive."

"Do you sleep with *any* men?"

"That's my business."

He looked at her critically. "I shouldn't be at all surprised if you were still a virgin. That's not a fashionable quality, you know."

"Nor am I a fashionable woman."

"Then you *are* a virgin!" When she made no answer he pursued: "Seriously, Anita, I find *you* attractive. I can think of no reason that you and I should not enjoy a discreet and decorous affair."

"There is no reason. Except that I do not wish it. Let's leave it at that, shall we? I find your company amusing. And I admire you professionally. Isn't that enough?"

"For a beginning, yes."

"Well, let us always be beginning."

"You'll go out with me again?"

"If you'll take me to a better place. We can go Dutch, if it's not too much better."

"Never! I'm an old-fashioned man."

"Which is why you want to seduce virgins, no doubt."

Carol's interest in her, not unsurprisingly, was stimulated by her resistance, so much so that she became apprehensive that he might infer that she was trying to allure him. She knew that the only effective step would have been to refuse to go out with him altogether, but she was afraid of incurring his terrible wrath, and besides, when he was not being libidinous, he could be extremely entertaining, and who else was making any effort to entertain her? On their next date he took her to a French restaurant in the East Fifties.

"I wonder if there's not something in your idea that every man, deep down, hankers for a virgin bride."

"I never expressed any such idea. There was no question of marriage that I remember in the relationship that you proposed."

"Ah, but if there *had* been?"

"But there wasn't. Nor was I looking for one."

"All right, then call it my idea. A virgin bride might have some of the charm of a new car. So many girls today have mileage."

After this, abruptly and much to her relief, he changed the subject, and for the rest of their very good meal he talked entrancingly about personalities at the museum. He knew everything about everyone and seemed perfectly willing to trust her with the most flagrant indiscretions. She would not have believed how much was going on under the dull, flat surface of cultural institutional life. But she could not help laughing, even when rather shocked, and when he took her home and did not even suggest that he should come upstairs for a nightcap, she allowed him to implant a warm, wet kiss on her still reluctant lips.

There were times now when he seemed almost content to let things go on indefinitely as they had been going, with a scholastic companionship at the office and an occasional "platonic" lunch or dinner. But he always insisted on paying for the latter, and she could not believe that a man so innately stingy would not expect an ultimate compensation. Sometimes, in his bad moods, he would wax so nasty as to seem to relieve her of the smallest obligation to him, but she had grown immune to the barbs of his wit, no matter how pointed and vile — and she knew that he knew this. He seemed to be counting on her being attracted to his very repulsiveness, and was he counting altogether in vain? She could not be sure. And there was another thing: she suffered from a sense of having beguiled him under false pretenses. For she was not, as she had half-implied, a virgin.

In graduate school she had had an affair that lasted a month with a fellow student, a pale, scrawny, oily-haired young man with a bad complexion and a desperate intensity, who had been distressingly open about wanting to prove to himself that he was not homosexual. They had confided everything about their unhappy childhoods to each other during sandwich lunches on park benches, and he had pounced on the idea that she too needed reassurance — reassurance that her feeling of rejection by her adoptive parents had not permanently frozen her in the conviction that she was impossible to love. Might they not each gain emotional emancipation by burning away the husk of a paralyzing neurosis in the deliberately kindled fire of sexual intercourse? And who was to say? Maybe they would find love, "true love," whatever that might be, while they were at it.

It was not a success for either, and they ended on a sorry note of mutual recrimination. Anita could not avoid considering the possible deduction that her suspicion of her own unlovableness might be more than a suspicion, as his, of his homosexuality, soon proved an exact prognostication. Was it not safer, was it not happier, was it not even nobler to relegate all thoughts of romance to the iron cupboard of fantasy, where, no matter how lurid, how throbbing with the unmentionable, the almost unthinkable, they could still be kept mysteriously uncontaminating and clean?

Carol embarked at length on a new tack. He urged her to introduce him to her family. For a while she resisted the idea, but at last, before a weekend that she was to spend with her mother, now married to a real estate broker in Rye, she agreed to let him come up on Sunday and drive her back to town. Supposing he found the family atmosphere as Babbitty as he undoubtedly expected he would? Would it not solve her problem? When she told her mother, the latter, delighted, insisted that Carol come for Sunday lunch.

The Tudor dormered house, the stepfather full of political and baseball chatter, the married stepbrothers and their spouses, so clean, immaculate, beaming, indifferent and unread, the spoiled, shouting children, seemed to be having the effect on the smiling and affable Carol that she had expected. Oh, she knew how to read behind his laughing eyes! But her mother seemed almost too tacky; it was a case of overkill. Her red hair was too red, her laugh too eager, her desire to show off her thin sprinkle of culture to a "real" museum curator too painfully evident. Obviously, she was intent on making up for three decades of benign neglect by charming "dear Dr. Sweeters" into marrying her waif.

Only when Carol had taken the family cat onto his lap and was stroking it did her mother sound a genuine note.

"Oh, you like cats, Dr. Sweeters? I can tell that by the way you stroke Dido. I always think it a sign of sensitivity and intelligence in a man to like cats. I suppose you have one at home?"

"I had one with me last summer for my vacation. In Newport."

"In Newport? Really? You go there? It must be so lovely. And I suppose you swim at Bailey's Beach and watch the tennis at the Casino?"

"My dear lady, I do no such things. I scamper like a mouse at the first approach of a member of what I call the leper colony. No, no, I rent for my scant month of freedom a tiny box of a house in the charming eighteenth-century section of Newport. There I and my cat dream of Rochambeau and Lafayette and walk to the old stone tower and pretend that the Vikings really built it, after all."

Anita glanced at her stepbrothers; of course they weren't listening.

"Lafayette?" her mother queried. "Did he spend his summers there?"

Anita had to say something. "What ever happened to your cat, Carol? Did it die?"

"Not that I know of. But I couldn't keep it in New York. I have no one to care for it when the museum sends me on trips."

"You left it with a friend?"

"I didn't know anyone who wanted it."

"Then what *did* you do with it?"

"I just left it."

"In the house?"

"Of course not." Carol began to show impatience. "I had to leave the house broom-clean. I left it outside."

"In the street?" Anita closed her eyes as her heart seemed to miss a beat. "You locked it out? Oh, Carol, you didn't! Tell me you didn't."

"What else was I to do?"

"But how was it to live?"

At this point her mother, sensing that the issue was becoming touchy, intervened. "Oh, cats are full of resources. It probably found mice and things."

"Lots of summer people do that," Anita's stepfather observed. "They buy a puppy or a kitten for the kiddies when they go to the lake and leave it there when it's time to go home."

"Leave it to starve!"

"Oh, Anita, you're just being dramatic," interposed the older stepbrother. "Meg and I did that with a cat in Vermont last summer. As Ma says, a cat can live off the land."

"I'd like to see you living off the land in Newport in the middle of winter!"

Anita said no more after this because she couldn't; it was as if she had turned into a pebble of muted horror in a puddle of alien frogs. Carol and her family seemed suddenly to belong to the same species of fauna; in such a jungle one could only yearn for the immunity of the inanimate. Carol, taking her silence as the signal they were through with a subject that was of no basic importance, proceeded to divert the table, even her brothers, with theories of why the civilization of the Mayas had crumbled so suddenly and inexplicably.

In the car going back to the city she complained of the onset of a migraine headache, and he switched on the radio for the

Philharmonic concert. When they heard the acrid blast of the *Boléro*, he offered to turn to a milder station, but she insisted that he leave it on, that it distracted her from the pain. And as her heart pounded to the throbbing rhythms, she closed her eyes for a vision of giddy reds and blacks alternating like a flashing night club sign in the empty dome of her mind and wondered whether she would not always loathe the man who was driving the car. At her house she fled without a word of thanks or farewell.

By the following day, after a night of sleepless reflection, she was ready for anything he could say to her. She was even ready for what he actually offered: a mock proposal of marriage. Of course it might even have been serious; she was well aware how necessary it was for him to screen his gravest intentions behind a bristling hedge of irony. He came to her little office and seated himself solemnly before her desk.

"Do you realize we have been acting out a novel, my dear Anita? And that truth is once again proven to be stranger than fiction? Only I had flattered myself that if such a thing happened to one so well read as I, it might be in the form of prose by Dostoyevski or Flaubert. But not at all. I find myself following the lines of the great Jane herself. It is in that favorite novel of the weaker sex, *Pride and Prejudice*, that I discover my banal little tale. For Darcy and Eliza agree no more about the vulgar Mrs. Bennet than you and I about the deplorable woman who is redeemed only by the good taste that she showed in choosing so rare a bundle from the adoption agency. Darcy looked with no more gloom at an alliance with Mrs. Bennet than I at one with your ma. But like him I must confess: 'In vain have I struggled . . . My feelings will not be repressed. You must allow me to tell you how ardently I admire and love you.' "

Anita found, despite her pounding heart, that she was able to fix her eyes with a newfound calmness on that sneering countenance. After a few moments she replied: "Let me answer you as if you were speaking in all seriousness. For I give you my solemn word that my response would be the same. I could never even think of marrying a man who could lock out in the cold the creature that had been his pet and friend."

Carol's high shriek of a laugh told her that her thrust had gone home. "You might at least reply to a joke with a joke!"

"If yours was a joke, so much the better. But I had rather make a fool of myself than leave you under a false impression. What I said I meant and shall always mean."

"Well, I guess unless the gods bring back that eminent cat lover and trainer Clyde Beatty, you are doomed to a life of chaste spinsterhood."

"That is my affair. And now, if you will forgive . . . "

But she knew, as he stamped out of the room, that he never would.

Communications between them thereafter were kept to a minimum. Anita made a particular point to report to him only when absolutely necessary, for he never lost the chance to denigrate either her work or her character or, if neither of these availed, her person. She could usually manage to scuttle away before the flash of his ugly temper came to the attention of others. But there was one terrible occasion when he took a revenge so cruel that she seriously considered resigning her post.

She happened to be studying the weird figures painted on the side of a Mayan pot, a new acquisition, when Carol walked in, purportedly to consult one of her books on pre-Columbian art, and peered over her shoulder. When he saw what she was looking at, he chuckled in a nasty way.

"Can you make out what he's doing?" He jabbed a finger at the male figure, whose beady eye and hooked nose suggested some organic connection with his eagle headdress.

"Doing? Is he doing anything?"

"Look at his hands."

"They seem to be in his lap."

Carol's laugh shrilled to a high cackle. "That is one way of putting it, I suppose. The way Anita Vogel *would* put it. But those hands, I'm afraid, are engaged in a good deal more than resting in his lap. Those hands are engaged, very neatly, in slitting his penis."

Anita started up in horror. "Oh, no!"

"Oh, yes, dear. We have excellent evidence that that is precisely what he is doing. And do you know what his lady consort is up to?" He paused while she stared at the pot as if he had turned it into a tarantula. "Well, *look,* silly."

"She seems to be pulling something out of her mouth."

"She is pulling a thorned rope through a hole that she has cut in her tongue."

Anita had to stifle a scream. "But how can they be doing such frightful things to themselves? They don't even seem to be suffering."

"Good point. We don't know why that is. Was it the artist's incapacity to depict suffering, or were the self-mutilators under drugs, or was it considered *lèse-majesté* to show royal persons in agony? For you understand, I'm sure, that what this lord and lady are doing was entirely voluntary. Indeed, it was considered one of the high privileges of their office. In the sacred ceremony of bloodletting the leaders of the nation were propitiating the gods for the benefit of their people. It was similar, of course, to our own deity assuming the crown of thorns and suffering the agony of the cross."

"And I thought theirs was a peaceful agrarian society," she murmured.

"How like you! You've been reading Morley, of course. Bowdlerized history. All that peace business has been long superseded. We now know the Mayas had one of the bloodiest civilizations known to history. Because they made war, not for defense or trade or territorial gain, but simply to collect captives to be sacrificed to their insatiable gods. It was not enough, you see, for them to mutilate themselves. They had to invade their neighbors to bring home victims to be castrated, disemboweled and then flung to the flames. Even in their sports they had to serve their hungry deities. The losing team of the ball game, their favorite sport, were sacrificed to the last man. It must have made for lively playing!"

"But you can't be sure of all that!"

"You mean *you* can't be sure of it, dear Anita. Because it doesn't fit in with your vision of the world as a flower garden where the devil himself is nothing worse than a man who abandoned his cat. Just take a look at this." He reached for one of the volumes on her desk, skipped through the pages of plates and slammed it down open before her. "You see that little carved figure of a naked man? He's a kind of box, really; he probably served as a reliquary. Something precious was kept in him, inserted through that hole in his belly. But he's not just a cute figurine *à la Chinoise*. He represents a sacrificial victim. Only this time the victim is not a stoical volunteer but a wretched captive. That is why his mouth is wide open, a black circle of shrieking agony. And why not? He has lost not only his genitalia but his intestines. We may safely assume that a merciful death spared him the final cruelty of the fire."

"Oh, please let me be!" Anita cried out, covering her ears. But she could still hear his satanic laugh as he left the room. She slammed the hateful book shut, but nothing, she knew, was ever going to erase that small figure from the flames Carol had lit in her morbid mind.

Of course, she could get no sleep that night, or even very much the night after. He had opened new depths of horror in the seemingly endless saga of man's inhumanity to man. It was one thing to have to contemplate histories where men killed for a purpose: for conquest or glory or even revenge; but here was something that had not existed even in the darkest chambers of her imagination. Here was a world where men existed *only* to kill; where wars were fought solely for that purpose; where daily life even in peacetime was subordinated to the ritual of bloodletting; where if you had not an enemy to butcher, you could only turn the knife of mayhem on yourself.

"Civilization!" she cried aloud, sitting up in bed and staring down at the moonlit, lamplit, yellow and milky street. "They call that a civilization! Better that it be obliterated from the books. Why even keep a record of it in a museum? Oh, but what does it matter? Are we any better, really?"

A morning came when she felt she simply could not go to work, and she called in sick. The next day she did the same thing, and the next. When the personnel director telephoned to ask whether she needed help, she invented family troubles and pleaded for a leave of absence; he offered her a week. The registrar, Miss Nesbit, a kindly soul who took a motherly interest in the women on the staff, rang up to ask if she might visit her, and Anita, distraught at the idea of seeing anyone, told her she was just on her way to Rye to stay with her mother. After that the telephone was silent, and she was free to spend her mornings in the park and her afternoons playing and replaying her few records. There were periods when she felt an odd lightness in her head and a painful heaviness in her feet.

I'm having a nervous breakdown! she thought in surprise. So *this* is what it's like.

In the middle of a cold and dripping afternoon her buzzer rang with a scaring loudness. She was at once convinced that it was Carol and knew that she couldn't see him. But the superintendent's voice announced the name of her visitor as something like "Speddon." Miss Speddon? How could Miss Speddon be coming to see her? Hers was more than a nervous breakdown. It had to be nearer insanity!

"Send her up," she muttered, and opened her door to watch

for the elevator. Could it be one of Carol's horrible jokes? She had met the lady only twice and then in the company of other staff members. Yet when the creaky gate opened, the grilled box disgorged, in a dripping red mackintosh and red hat absurdly like a fireman's, none other than the great collector herself.

"My dear Miss Vogel, I hear you've been ill. Miss Nesbit saw you in the park from her window yesterday, and she was concerned, because you had said you were going to your mother's. She did not know quite what to do, so I told her I'd drive by your house on my way home and see for myself whether there was anything you needed. May I come in and have a little chat with you? You do look pulled down, my child. I'm afraid you're going to have to let someone take care of you."

Such was the old lady's gift of inspiring confidence that fifteen minutes later they were seated comfortably by the stove drinking orange juice. Anita felt it was all very unreal but also very wonderful.

"Now that we have been over the preliminaries, and you see that I am not an interfering ogress," Miss Speddon was saying, "and now that I see you haven't, thank the Lord, incurred any dangerous illness, I wonder if you would allow me to be a little more personal? I cannot help feeling that the staff of my beloved museum are a kind of family of mine."

"Oh, please, Miss Speddon, be as personal as you choose. I cannot imagine anything more flattering."

"Well, then, I'll be bold. You must know by now that in small institutions like ours everybody butts into everyone else's business. Miss Nesbit thought you might have had a falling-out with Dr. Sweeters over his mistreatment of a cat. Could that be so?"

"He locked it out to starve! His own pet! Because he couldn't be bothered to find a home for it. Oh, Miss Speddon, please don't try to reconcile us! I didn't really like him anyway, but now I find him loathsome."

"My dear, I wouldn't think of it. It was a cruel and vicious thing for him to do, and I quite agree with your assessment of his character. No, what brought me here was the idea, suggested by what Miss Nesbit told me, that there might be a bond between you and me."

Anita wondered whether her mild dizziness was not simply a natural reaction to the charm of this wonderful old woman. She didn't wish her ever to stop talking; she wanted to drink orange juice and listen to her consoling words till doomsday.

"I suspect that what we may really have in common is an overdeveloped sympathy for suffering persons. I say overdeveloped because it does not do either the sufferers or ourselves much good. But there we are — we're stuck with it. When I was a young woman, about your age, I wanted to go abroad in the Great War to work in a hospital. I wasn't a nurse, but I was willing to do any kind of dirty work. My father was a man of considerable influence, and he was able to arrange it for me. He warned me gravely that the shock of what I was going to see might be almost fatal to one of my sensitivity, but he qualified this by adding: 'Daisy, it may also be the making of you. You're too timid about life. You've been a wonderful companion to me since your mother died, and we've had a great time roaming the world together and collecting beautiful things. But I've been selfish. I've let myself monopolize your life, I've probably prevented you from marrying.' He hadn't, but there was no persuading him of this. 'All along,' he said, 'I've been waiting for the appearance of a real love in your life. When that happened I vowed that I was not going to stand between you and it. Of course, I thought it would come in the shape of a man, and I was determined not to be small or snobbish about him. Well, it seems I was wrong. It wasn't a man at all. Your love has come in the shape of a mission. Maybe you will see things that you cannot endure. But I have sworn to myself, and I must stand by my oath. Go and God be with you!'

"Well, my dear, I went, trembling. And I did well to tremble. I am not going to tell you what I saw in France. Suffice it to say that my reason might have tottered had I not had so much hard work to do. Blood and bedpans can save the mind. It was the coming home on the boat, after the Armistice, that was the hardest part. Then I had the nightmare of memory with no distraction, and looking over the cold, broad, tossing Atlantic was no comfort. I can understand why two friends of mine, twin sisters, leaped to their deaths from another returning vessel. I was sorely tempted to do the same. But I resisted, and when I was home again my dear old father helped me to recover. That is another reason I came to you today: I understand you are not close to either of your parents. I do not know what I should have done at that time without the one I still had. Father took me firmly in hand and told me to fill my eyes and mind with beautiful things. He taught me to accept the ugliness of human nature by concentrating on the beautiful art man could create. Augustus, he would say, might have slaughtered in war thousands of his fellow mortals, but he left Rome a city of gleaming marble. Wagner might have been a megalomaniac and an anti-Semite, but we have *Parsifal* and *Tristan*. You may find it curious that he should have sought to save my soul with material things, that he should have offered me objects in place of ideas, but it worked. I've had a happy life, my dear."

And in the ensuing months Miss Speddon proceeded, in her own grave, imperturbable way, to supply Anita with one of her own. She persuaded her to take a longer leave of absence from the museum and to move out of her apartment into 36th Street, where she could be more comfortably looked after until she should have recovered her spirits. The visit proved to both that the bond between them was no figment of Miss Speddon's imagination, but a very real and durable thing, and Anita agreed at last to live permanently with her new patroness and to go back to the museum, when she ultimately did, in the new and grander role of curator of the Speddon collection.

She found herself so happy, and in so amazingly short a time, that she gratefully resolved to devote all her energies and actions henceforth to the perfecting of the role of acolyte at this new altar. It was not long before she actually exulted at having no life or friends of her own. Miss Speddon made strong, periodic objections to this, but she was old and waxing feebler by the month, and it was only natural that she should at last accept the ministrations of this efficient, understanding young woman who showed temper only when resisting any proposal that she do aught but live for the benefit of her hostess. To Anita it was as if this benign, elderly angel had winged her way down into the cavernous shadows of her bleak old life, as in a romantic engraving by Gustav Doré, and borne her back up to an alabaster paradise of trumpets and halos.

What did she need of her old world? What, for that matter, did she need of anyone's? Miss Speddon's decorous, antique society, largely female and widowed or virginal, soft, silent and gently smiling, accepted her as they would have any discreet, well-mannered young woman who had come to act as "Daisy's" paid companion. On nights when Miss Speddon ventured into society alone, Anita would stay home and wait for her return, for all the world like a faithful dog.

At the museum it was understood that she was now responsible directly to Miss Speddon, who paid her salary. She never thrust her opinions on her patroness, whom she accompanied on all her buying expeditions, but when asked, she would reply succinctly and to the point, and so developed, without seeking it, a definite influence over the collection. She even managed to trim some of Miss Speddon's sentimental extravagances, particularly in the area of native crafts. For if the old lady, in art and sculpture, had a fine if conservative taste, she was inclined to purchase with too heavy a hand the quaint produce of old villages and farms: quilts, weather vanes, grilled fences, andirons, duck decoys, pots, pans, tea kettles and the like. It sometimes seemed that in buying artifacts to trace the history of America she was trying to buy America itself.

Anita loved everything about the life at 36th Street. Even its rigid regularity was agreeable to her. Meals were always at precisely the same time; Monday nights were for the opera, Thursdays for the concert; on Wednesdays there was apt to be a small, stately dinner at home. Weekends were passed in the large stone mansion in Fairfield, where Anita would walk in the garden or the bit of wood, or read. She found that she was becoming even more methodical than her hostess, that she minded the smallest variation in the routine. She had at last succeeded in building the stout and durable wall that seemed able to hold her old anxieties at bay. It would protect her both day and night; there was hardly a chink in it except the one through which Carol Sweeters's mocking face occasionally peered. At last she did not mind even him. She discontinued her visits to her parents, who were willing enough to forget about her. Her fortress was ready, her drawbridge up, and she was prepared to pour down boiling oil on any who dared to scale the ramparts. Within, on an emerald greensward, she could sit safely with Evelyn Speddon. She was perfectly secure. She was almost perfectly happy.

And then Mark Addams came to the museum.

3

IN HER three conventual years at 36th Street Anita had learned to exercise a tight control over vagrant sexual attractions. At "home," as she now called Miss Speddon's residences in town and country, there was little enough to disturb her, and at the museum her sober deportment and dutiful industriousness had done little to allure her fellow workers. But it took more than this to exempt her mind from the intrusion of male images. What she taught herself to do when one of these threatened to fix itself more than briefly in her reflections was to create the mental drama of a romantic relationship, deliberately converting mere possibilities into vibrant but nonetheless transient fictions. This happened with one of the younger trustees, who chose to make it his particular function to become thoroughly familiar with the Speddon collection, and again with a handsome accountant with whom she had to work on the insurance problems raised by the theft of an important artifact. Both were married men; neither had the smallest apparent biological interest in her; but their imagined counterparts could be briefly diverting and ultimately dismissed. And her little games went far to reinforce the old conclusion that she was never going to attract the kind of man that attracted her. Which was just as well, anyway, was it not, if she had resolved to dedicate her life to better things?

Mark Addams, however, was different. Not only was he permanently present, having to walk by her office door several times a day to his own at the end of the corridor; he took a persistent, friendly, rather jovial interest in her. It was not, certainly, a romantic interest — he had plenty of that outside the office — but he had a way of seeming playfully to imply it was a pity that it wasn't. She had never had to cope with anything quite like this before, and her heart let her down by quivering outrageously whenever he addressed her as "Pal."

The trouble was that even their slight actual relationship was not so utterly remote from the fantasy that she defensively constructed around it as had been the fairy tales she had fabricated of the trustee and the accountant. About Mark she had invented the fable that the acting director, crushed by his failure to win the permanent post and abandoned by the crude lawyer lover whose greedy heart yearned only for success, had turned in his desolation to a more sympathetic heart. Now, however ridiculous this was, it was not inconceivable that Mark should be passed over for the directorship, and Anita had recently heard rumors that all might not be well between him and his girl friend. She even seemed — however much the idea alarmed her — to make out a correlation between the cheerful note of Mark's address and the warm words that he used in her imagination. Suppose — a panic-making thought — she should lose her mental balance and betray her preoccupations by some blabbed, involuntary remark to him? Would he not then, like Hippolytus hearing the shameful confession of his infatuated stepmother, draw back in horror and shock?

When Miss Speddon informed her on a Monday evening

when she returned from work that she had invited Mr. Addams to dinner and the opera that very night, Anita in dismay was about to plead a headache, and checked herself only when she realized that this might be interpreted as too great rather than too small an interest in the prospective guest. And so an hour later, washed and dressed but miserably tense, she found herself alone with Mark in the parlor. Miss Speddon never appeared at cocktails, staying in her room until dinner was announced. Mark, of course, was as much at ease as Anita was not. Glass in hand, he roamed the long dusky chamber, surveying with a critical but admiring eye the portraits on the walls — a Gilbert Stuart, a Rembrandt Peale, two Copleys — and the vast Frederick Church panorama of the Amazon, which seemed to open the end wall into a glorious window on wide dark water and thick dark foliage.

"How wonderful to live with these things!" he exclaimed. "To be surrounded by them, to be a part of them. To be eaten up by them! And, my God, look at that vase! It's early Ming, isn't it? Why, there's a whole set of them."

The pictures were lit, as were the cabinets, but on the tables in the corners it was not easy to make out each object.

"I can turn on more lights."

"Don't! It's more mysterious like this. I think, if I were Miss Speddon, I'd be perfectly happy!"

"But you live all day with beautiful things, Mark."

"Ah, but I have to share them with the public! With the staff. They're all ticketed and classified. Here they'd just be mine." He turned, grinning, to clench and unclench his fists, mimicking a miser. "They'd have no function beyond my personal edification. Oh, yes, I think to be rich would be to be perfectly happy. I'd trade places with Miss Speddon tomorrow."

"And be an old woman instead of a young man? And infirm instead of the picture of health?"

"The infirmity would not be so good, I grant. But I shouldn't mind the age or even the sex so long as I had a couple of years to enjoy these things. What's time, after all? Don't we measure life by intensity?"

"Of course you're not serious."

"Do you know I almost am, Anita?" he responded in a tone that at least simulated earnestness. He came over to sit on the divan beside her. "There are times when I wonder if our game is worth the candle. The whole business of storing and cataloguing and exhibiting beautiful objects. When the only way to take them in is to live with them, as you do."

"But I don't own them."

"Don't you, in a way? Haven't you made them yours? There's something about you, Anita, just sitting there, so quietly, so serenely, that makes me sense you have absorbed these things in a way I could never hope to in my crazy life."

"I'm not absorbing anything that you're not."

"Oh, but you are!" He leaned forward to stare boldly into her eyes. "You're quite wonderful, Anita. You really are. The rest of us just exist. You live."

"Oh, Mark, you're so ridiculous." She turned away from him with a shudder. And then suddenly she was almost angry. How dared he play with her so? She faced him now with a kind of defiance. "What about Miss Norton? Doesn't *she* live?"

He drew back, startled. Was he going to be Hippolytus, after all? But then he seemed suddenly to decide to take her question seriously. "Do you know, that's just what she doesn't do? It's law, law, law, all day and all night. I don't like to sound like a chauvinist pig, but there's something about litigation that seems to coarsen a woman. I don't know how much longer I can take Chessie's long hours and preoccupation with becoming a partner. And even if she does, will it make that much difference? The partners in her sweatshop work just as hard."

"Sweatshops, dear me! I hope you're not talking about the

museum. The temperature would hardly be the thing for my paintings."

They both turned to the door, where their smiling hostess was standing, waiting to lead them down to dinner.

The opera was *Siegfried,* and they were only four in Miss Speddon's box. Mrs. Kay, a widow, tiny, old and exquisite, with neatly waved snowy hair and an air of tranquil, friendly composure which nothing could ruffle, had been waiting for them when they arrived, belonging, as she explained to Mark, to the "Asbestos Club" of those who always arrived before that canopy was lifted. Unlike most of Miss Speddon's friends, she was the mother of three middle-aged sons, all notably successful in different professions, and she was considered a font of practical wisdom by those who came to 36th Street.

Anita paid scant attention to the activities of the hero and dwarf in the first act; her mind was too full of a possible breakup between Mark and his girl friend. Her fantasy seemed to be growing out of control; like a malignant chest tumor it threatened to break the rib cage. She even wondered if Miss Speddon's old waitress had not put something in her cocktail. Could she be sure that she had heard Mark correctly? Wasn't it the Chessie Norton of her fantasy, and not the real one, whom she had heard him describe? Closing her eyes in agitation, she tried to let the music distract her.

When the lights went up for the intermission, Miss Speddon rose and gave her arm to Mark. She usually took a stroll with Anita between the first and second acts, but when the latter rose to follow, Mrs. Kay touched her arm.

"Stay with me, my dear. There's something I have to tell you."

Alone in the box with Mrs. Kay, Anita, surprised and faintly apprehensive, waited for the old lady to speak, gazing down over the packed aisles of risen people below. The last members of the orchestra were disappearing under the stage.

Still Mrs. Kay did not speak, and the tiny smile on her thin lips had shrunk suddenly to a crisp line.

"It's something rather serious, I'm afraid," she said at last. "Our friend is gravely ill."

Anita's first reaction was how odd it was she should not be more surprised. Her lips formed the almost voiceless answer: "How ill?"

"As ill as can be. It's her heart, and nothing can be done about it. She may leave us any time. The only thing Dr. Craven is sure of is that it can't be long."

Anita clutched for the railing of the box. "Why are you telling me this? And why now?" She opened her mouth as if to cry out, but she didn't.

Mrs. Kay scrutinized her. "Do you want to go home, dear, and weep? Or do you want to show the character of which both Daisy and I are sure you are capable? Oh, I know it's hard for the young to face death. You don't see it in your mirror every morning."

"But why here, of all places?" Anita repeated, anguished now. "Miss Speddon may be back any moment."

"Not until the curtain. She has arranged that with me. It was entirely her idea. She wants you to be prepared, but not to discuss it with her. Death, she believes, should be a private affair. When she comes back, she will press your hand, and that will be all. She is counting on you to be very brave. And to look after her things."

"And she will not count on me in vain," Anita murmured. For just a second she allowed herself the indulgence of covering her face with her hands. Then she turned back to Mrs. Kay. "I'm all right now. Tell me more about it."

As Mrs. Kay, in her low, measured tones, proceeded to explain the exact state of Evelyn Speddon's degenerating heart, Anita found her mind as much a jumble of jarring thoughts as there were noises from the chattering auditorium below. Something seemed to want to escape from that mind; it was as if she had to close every aperture, pressing down with imagined fingers on its roof to keep enclosed the notion that what went on there was only her own business, that that dark cavern hid an amorality only blameless if never translated into words or deeds. For otherwise what would become of a soul that felt a wicked thrill at the intrusion of action into an existence so stale? Was the curtain about to rise on a drama in her own life, as it was about to rise on the second act of Wagner's music drama? And did poor Miss Speddon have to perish for Anita's liberty, her distraction, her libidinous fantasies? Surely such an Anita had to be a monster, even if she kept the knowledge to herself!

"Here they come now," Mrs. Kay was saying, and Anita jumped up as her patroness, with a gravely inquiring look, stepped into the box and took her hand to give it a quick, tight squeeze before taking her seat. Anita, returning that squeeze, said nothing and looked nothing, but hurriedly took her own place in the second row. But she had noted for the first time the glaze of death on those long gray cheeks.

The lights dimmed, and she listened to Mark, who was murmuring something facetious about the dragon soon to be felled by the hero. She shuddered in unutterable dismay at her mental picture of Mark, clad in a bearskin, approaching her poor patroness with the gleaming Nothung in his murderous hand.

4

MARK ADDAMS, contrary to what was generally believed by the staff of the museum, was by no means assured of the board's vote for the directorship, and nobody was more aware of this than he. He had the backing of the powerful chairman, which might have been sufficient for any other position on the staff, but even docile trustees have a way of showing surprising independence when it comes to the selection of a chief executive officer, and Mark had to contend with what the second ranking board member, Peter Hewlett, termed his "academic nudity." Mark had a B.A. from Bowdoin, where he had majored in history of art, but no master's or doctor's degree. After college he had gone into advertising and from there into a public relations firm, and it was as a rising young officer in charge of fund-raising for the Museum of North America that he had first come to the attention of Sidney Claverack.

Working congenially together, the two had managed to double the institution's endowment, and Claverack, delighted with the man he now chose to regard as his protégé, had contributed his own money to make possible Mark's employment as "assistant director in charge of development" at a salary equal to what Mark's firm had been paying him and actually in excess of that of the about-to-retire director, who was sixty-five and suffering from emphysema.

"I'm going to put all my cards on the table," Claverack had said to him. "I don't mind telling you that you seem to be just what I've been looking for as director of this shop. I haven't made it exactly a secret that I'm not too keen about the available candidates in the field. No matter how much they prate about their administrative abilities, they don't strike me as being nearly on a par with men who've been out in the big hard world of business competition. And yet museums have become big business, and they've got to be run accordingly. Not that I minimize the artistic function. Perish the thought! I have no idea of throwing out the baby with the bath water. But what I really want — and what I hope I can persuade my board to accept — is a man who can sell a product as well as buy one. I know you can sell this institution. You've already proved that. Hell, what more does a museum need? Somebody who can tell you how many angels can stand on the head of a pin or how many choirboys Michelangelo buggered? Fella, you're the answer to a maiden's prayer. Not that I'm exactly a maiden."

Mark had prided himself on being nobody's fool. He had suspected that behind the chairman's pale, smiling face, behind the large, commanding nose, the sleek black hair and watery blue eyes, behind the whole vigorous, alert and well-tailored figure, there probably existed a spirit of ruthlessness and inexorable advantage-seeking. Sidney Claverack was one of those men who never had to raise his voice, though Mark was sure that he could if he had to. His charm, his wit and his innate reasonableness, his gentle, ineluctable, pulverizing reasonableness ("You *do* agree with me, old man, don't you? I knew you would") could be counted on to bring one around, while the heavier ordnance was left unused in his arsenal, though not to rust there, never to be allowed to rust there. For there just always might be somebody who simply would not be convinced that the present power structure was the right one, for the arts as well as for business, or who stubbornly refused to be persuaded that the man who could not give the public what it wanted — or what its public relations counsel told it to want — was a fool who had no place either as an agent or beneficiary of philanthropy. But Mark's business had always been precisely to deal with such public fiduciaries as Sidney. He had to know what he was about.

He also knew that Sidney was a new but increasingly familiar type of trustee in the world of the cultural institution. Instead of devoting his primary ambition to his own business, like the older generation of museum sponsors, and giving his not-for-profit wards simply the benefit of his disinterested wisdom and money, he had left the management of his law firm, in which he had early achieved the first position, to his younger partners and gone on to identify the Museum of North America with himself. It had not, it was true, been his first choice. The United States Senate had been his earlier and perhaps more appropriate goal, but he had lost the race to a Democratic opponent after the expenditure by his backers of so vast a campaign fund that he had not deemed it feasible to raise another. And then, resolutely, spiritedly, he had turned the prow of his battle cruiser to the harbor of the visual arts.

Nor did Mark see anything wrong with this. Why should the arts not be entitled to the best from the world of entrepreneurs? Had not Sidney Claverack put together for his own account a distinguished collection of modern American paintings? Was it not his avowed intention to quadruple the endowment of the museum and bring its attendance to fourth in the city, conceding only the unchallengeable supremacy of the Met, the Modern and the Natural History? When Carol Sweeters had pointed out to Mark that in a recent show of Canadian art at the museum, Claverack had managed to slip in an undue number of canvases by a young painter whose works in his own collection might be expected to appreciate in value by the association, Mark had put it down to that curator's well-known habit of denigrating his superiors.

When the ailing director had retired, after Mark had been in office only a year, he was named acting head, pending the decision of the committee of trustees appointed to find a successor. Of course this had aroused considerable resentment in the museum: a clique of older curators were never going to regard Mark as anything other than an upstart and the sidekick of an officious chairman of the board. But Mark knew that time was on his side and that many of the younger staff members already regarded him as the Galahad on whom they could count to pull the institution out of its doldrums and safeguard their own futures and pensions.

These latter were not content to let the museum remain a quiet, sleepy organization where the older curators, absorbed in the cultivation of their individual gardens, tended to resent the intrusion of the public and to regard a strike by guards and maintenance men as a bonanza that would turn the building into a silent haven for scholars. The juniors were eager to follow Mark's lead and turn the museum into a kind of graduate school for all ages whose artifacts would offer instruction in the history and culture of a continent, whose shop would be filled with enticing aids to learning and whose great central gallery would be available to display any of the popular visiting "megashows" so heavily covered by the press. By day the halls would be filled with students; by night they would glitter with benefit parties. Attendance was the new god at whose shrine Mark worshiped, and why not? What would be the good of a museum in the middle of a desert?

But if the younger staff members optimistically and naïvely

believed that the search committee would automatically follow the guidance of its chairman, Mark, less sanguine, realized that their failure to do so (and who could tell if the fickle Claverack might not be persuaded to change his mind or even sponsor a new favorite?) would deprive him of his one chance to achieve the first position in a major museum. For what was an "academic nude" without Sidney Claverack, and where else was he going to find such a sponsor? If the board didn't choose him, he could only go back to his old public relations firm — if indeed they still wanted him.

And if indeed he wanted to go back. Mark had always dreamed of a career that would combine material prosperity with eminence in a cultural field. At college he had wanted first to be an actor, then an artist, then a writer; but always a shrewd assessor of his own abilities, he had early divined that he was not destined to achieve high rank as servant of any of those muses. Yet his faith that he had an unusual gift, if he could only find the muse to bring it out, had never wavered. In the State House in Augusta, the home town where his father ran a small pharmaceutical business, there was a portrait gallery where the primitive likenesses of early hirsute legislators were startlingly dominated by the painting of a lady in flowing white, holding a golden goblet in outstretched hands, her mouth an oval of utterance, presumably of some strong and noble song. It was the diva Lillian Nordica, a daughter of Maine, depicted in her greatest role, Isolde. Mark had vowed that he would stand out as much from his contemporaries as the Wagnerian soprano stood out from all those worthy senators and assemblymen.

And in his first two years at the museum it had begun to look as if he might achieve his goal. It had even seemed appropriate to him that the happiness he felt in the evolution of his professional life should have been complemented by a corresponding development in his private one. It was again through Sidney Claverack that blessings seemed to flow, for he met Chessie Norton, an associate in the latter's law firm, at a cocktail party given in the chairman's Park Avenue apartment. It was true that this tall redhead had not at first struck him as a blessing — rather the reverse, in fact.

"I guess I don't believe much in museums," she had retorted in a snooty drawl when he had inquired if she was familiar with his and their host's institution. "I find myself pitying the poor pictures on the walls. Think of all the crap they must have to hear about themselves!"

"That is, I grant, a sobering thought. But how else are we to educate the public?"

"How do you imagine you're doing that?"

"By teaching it to appreciate beautiful things."

"Oh, bushwa. Can you really believe that? The only way to appreciate a beautiful painting is to learn how to paint. I don't say you have to paint well. Only enough to see what it's all about."

"Would you say that of all the arts? Sculpture? Music? Writing?"

"I would."

He reflected that she seemed horribly sure of herself. "And what about the people already educated? Doesn't a museum offer them something?"

"Well, it offers them more, certainly. But aren't we reaching the point where reproductions will do the trick just as well?"

"Never!"

"I'll bet I could fool you on a lot of stuff in your own shop. Didn't Boldini's father paint half the Rembrandts at the Met?"

"If he did, he was a greater painter than Rembrandt."

The redhead seemed somewhat appeased by this. "Well, at least you're not an authenticity buff. As if it mattered who painted what!"

After this they chatted more easily. She showed no inclination to talk to anyone else at the party, even though some of her law associates were present, and Mark tried to interpret this as an interest in himself rather than a general indifference. Perhaps it was because of the intent way she had of attending to each question he put, a habit that, after all, she might simply have acquired in court. Still, there was something about her that belied her apparently assumed detachment, that suggested it was more armor than soul. The topic of museums led to that of curators and then to problems of administration and at last to the law and her own life. When he asked her to dine with him, she accepted as casually as if they had been fellow clerks leaving the office for lunch. As she seemed to care just as little where they went, he guided her to the nearest restaurant, a rather shabby Italian one on Third Avenue.

At their table she seemed to relax and drank a considerable amount of Chianti. At first she had reminded him of a Modigliani model, long and lank, with long red hair, small, rather staring eyes and a twisted slot of a mouth over an oval chin, which, when lifted, enhanced her sometime air of hypercriticism. But as she became animated and enthusiastic, if a trifle too brisk, energy seemed to ripple through her, sending ardor into her long pale cheeks and flashes into her cold green eyes. There were moments when she could be almost beautiful.

A discussion of the turbulence of the nineteen sixties led him to inquire whether her interest in law had exempted her from the radical activities of that time.

"Quite the contrary," she replied, with a slight quickening of interest. "You might even say I was 'all out.' I'm afraid it's a dreary and typical tale."

"I'd like to hear it."

"Would you really?" She studied him for a moment and then nodded, as if to indicate he had passed muster. "My poor parents! But then I suppose it was the same thing for many of their generation. There they were, in their nice little Queen Anne house in Darien, with two cars and a country club and just what everyone wanted in the way of family, a boy and a girl, almost the same age. Dad — you guessed it — was a vice-president of America Bank, and Mother had her garden club. Bruce was at Yale, and I at Vassar, and all was for the best in the best of all possible worlds."

"Until pot and sex and war."

She gravely assented. "Until all of those things. Except with Bruce, pot led to cocaine. He protested, he marched, he smashed windows — as I did — as we all did — until we became disillusioned with disillusionment. Bruce held a news conference in New Haven and announced that he was going to kill himself."

"Which of course he didn't."

"Which of course he did." A spark in Chessie's eyes seemed to reprove him for daring to question the dark integrity of the Nortons. "He shot himself in our cellar in Darien. Dad could never understand or cope with it. He turned away, refused to talk about it. Mother was worse and yet better. In time I came to think her quite wonderful. 'Bruce has made his choice,' she told me. 'There is a kind of relief to it, in the end. He didn't have the will to live, so he had to die. It should be easier now for the rest of us. For me anyhow. For I've decided to live!' "

Mark divined that the only way to respond to this was in the same tone. The girl would have spurned any expression of sympathy in which her ringing hammer detected the smallest pitch of falseness. But didn't such hammers have a way of creating the very falseness they were looking for?

"And that helped you? Her Spartan attitude?"

"Ultimately. It also helped me accept how soon Bruce was forgotten. I saw why some people make a cult of the dead. It's the only way to avoid total oblivion. And maybe the dead should be forgotten. When I saw how utterly all the protesting of the sixties was swept under the rug, when I saw that I was turning from a would-be martyr to a by-passed crank, I decided to follow Mother and live. I resolved to fight only for things that I personally cared about. A personal interest gives you direction and push and hate." Chessie's stare was now illuminated as if by a small flame. "I wanted to be a lawyer, and I wanted to end discrimination against women in law firms and courtrooms. Well, I and my likes have just about done it!"

It excited him to feel that she too could be excited. "So now that battle is won, what remains? To become a partner and make a lot of money? Maybe a judge?"

Her repeated study of his countenance seemed to seek further assurance that he was not laughing at her. Again she nodded. "Something like that."

"What about marriage and a family? Or is that too Darien?"

"I haven't ruled them out."

"I'm glad to hear that."

She didn't smile. "I haven't ruled anything out, Mark Addams."

Indeed she had not, for their relationship almost at once developed into the affair that had now lasted for more than two years. Chessie continued to resent men in general and Mark, in some respects, in particular — she persisted in dubbing him a sentimentalist who was much too keen about many matters that she regarded as trivial — but she was under no misapprehension as to the importance of a man in her life. When their affair started, he had imagined it was going to be largely a physical one, to which he had no objection, but he had soon discovered that the sexual act was the prelude to the unfolding of some unexpected aspects of her personality. When Chessie's major suspicions of his male chauvinism were overcome, she became a congenial and sympathetic friend. If she worked as hard as ever in the office, she devoted most of her free time to him, and she manifested a zeal for plays, operas, concerts and even museums that he had not suspected to exist behind the façade she had first presented of a rather languid disenchantment. Chessie had been deeply hurt by her brother and by her own disappointments, and she was leery of being hurt again, but she still had a sharp appetite for life.

Was she in love? Was *he*? He sometimes suspected that the only thing that held him back was his fear that she might make fun of him as being old-fashioned. He knew that it was perfectly possible, even normal, in their day and age, for a young and healthy woman to be indefinitely, perhaps permanently, satisfied with a relationship that did not offer the security of marriage (if such security still existed) or the fulfillment of children (if they still fulfilled). Chessie was certainly unlike what his mother had regarded as a womanly woman. She did not seem to believe in any future at all — except in that partnership in Sidney Claverack's firm.

And when she did at last advert to the subject of marriage, it was distasteful to him. This was only because of the way she put it. They had been staying in a ski lodge in Vermont, and after a wonderful day on the slopes, at dinner, almost as if she were turning reluctantly to a rather tedious duty after an irresponsible but delightful holiday, she said abruptly: "You know, if we're ever going to get married, we should be thinking about it now. After all, I'm thirty-one, and the women in my family have a history of early menopause."

He replied, after a moment of reflection, with an evasion: "Is that what Juliet whispered to Romeo from the balcony?"

"All right, forget it!" She was instantly irate. "It's not going to be said of me that I threw myself at a man."

"I can guarantee that."

"The next move, if any, will have to come from you."

"I'll check with Ma and see if our men have a record of early impotence."

"Very funny."

"Seriously, Chessie, I'm not closing my mind on this issue."

It struck him now that he never called her "dearest" or "darling."

"But maybe someone else is."

"Oh, come off it, Chessie. It isn't like you to be so easily hurt. Can't a man be as businesslike as a woman? Must I be sloppily romantic while you're bleakly down to earth?"

She shrugged impatiently. "It's all such crap. Let's get back to the way we were. That was much better."

And she proceeded to do just that. It was one of the things that was so amazing about her. She was as cheerful for the rest of the evening as he had ever seen her. But there was no question of any lovemaking that night.

5

IT WAS certainly not the best thing for his relationship with Chessie that museum events should have drawn him into greater intimacy with Anita Vogel at just this time. Sidney Claverack was doing over Miss Speddon's will — an annual procedure — and he summoned Mark to his law office to discuss the matter with a candor that even then struck the younger man as out of place in an attorney supposedly wholeheartedly devoted to his client's interests.

"She doesn't really trust me. Even though I'm her cousin, and my family has represented her forever. But then she doesn't really trust anybody. She's hell-bent to tie up her money till the trumpet of the last judgment. But she likes *you*, Mark. She thinks you're fresh and clean and idealistic and all that crap. You'd better work on that, fella. Go and see her. Talk to her about the dead hand sitting too heavily on the living."

"You mean talk to her about her will? How would I dare bring the subject up?"

"You won't have to. She will. She can't talk to anyone from the museum for fifteen minutes without bringing it up."

"But wouldn't she think it impertinent if I made suggestions? And wouldn't it be?"

Sidney paused, as if to find how best to bring home to this young man the gravity of the matter. "Mark, listen to me. That woman's fortune is the break our museum has been waiting for ever since its foundation. It's the windfall that should put us at last right up there on top with the great museums of this country. But what good will her dough do us if it's all tied up in crazy old maid knots? You've got to get in there and fight. Fight for your company's chance to take its proper rank in the world. And, all right, fight for the old girl, too, if it makes you feel any better. I mean fight for her *real* best interests — if she'll only see what they are and stop being such a nanny goat." He paused, perhaps sensing he had gone too far. "Let's put it this way, my friend. You convince Daisy Speddon to leave us her money and collection without crippling conditions, and I'll convince the board to name you director. Claim it of me! There's not a trustee, including old Peter Hewlett, who wouldn't bow to a coup like that. Hell, man, you wouldn't even need your B.A., let alone a master's!"

Mark didn't need anything beyond these magic words to go to work. The very next day he embarked on a campaign of cultivating his friendship with Anita Vogel. It was obvious that she offered him the most available key to her patroness's mind and heart. Nor did it take him long to convert this hitherto casual and rather bantering relationship into one considerably deeper. Indeed, the friendship soon threatened to get out of his control. Mark had not previously suspected how much this tense creature fancied him, and he was amused and intrigued by the interest that she obviously and unsuccessfully tried to conceal. It was not so much that he suspected himself of returning this interest as that the contrast between her virginal isolation from the world and his own perhaps undue involvement with it made him think of himself as a kind of savage Gaul and of her as a Roman Vestal. Her deep concern with beautiful things, and unconcern with every conceivable norm and standard of his own busy life, had their attraction for him at a time when Claverack's world had begun to seem too worldly, its rush too rushing. Might there not be a balm for him in the very commotion of Anita's concentrated whirlpool, particularly if he were the cause of its swirling? She gave him the impression that if she ever should turn her attention from Miss Speddon's pots and pans to a man, it would be a total transference. And that might be a sufficiently pleasant experience for the man, particularly if that man was a bit tired of being only a part of the life and career of Miss Chessie Norton.

The latter, who had met Anita at the museum and again at Miss Speddon's when she was assisting Mr. Claverack with the famous will, promptly flared the cause of her lover's preoccupation.

"I shouldn't be at all surprised if you didn't imagine yourself a kind of Colonel Higginson discovering Emily Dickinson," she suggested bleakly one evening when he had commented too keenly on Anita's extreme devotion to her job. They had gone the previous Saturday night to a play about the Amherst poetess. "You think you may be the man who will bring her out. Big, brave, wonderful, condescending you! But there's one little difference. Emily was a genius, and Miss Vogel is a drip. So that even if you're as opaque as Higginson, it will make just as little matter. Emily remained a genius in spite of him. Miss Vogel will remain a drip in spite of you."

When Chessie was nasty, she reminded him again uncomfortably of that Modigliani model. At such moments he could actually dislike her.

"I wonder if Anita *isn't* a bit of a genius," he parried. "If you had lived more with Titians and less with torts, you might have learned to appreciate people who don't happen to believe that lawyers are the be-all and end-all of life. Or that the greatest goal of man isn't necessarily to slip off with the moneybags under a squid spray of small print."

"Oink, oink! Do I hear the chauvinist pig grunting? We girls know that ploy. How to keep a woman out of the market-place by turning her into a Vestal. And then tossing her the rag of aloofness to cover the bare ass of her servitude!"

Nothing could have pushed him more towards Anita than Chessie's meanness, particularly when she seemed to divine his own fantasies. If she chose to create a rival for herself by placing Anita in the compound of victims of the male, she might be building more dangerously than she knew. Mark was beginning to wonder if he could not make out the loss of a feminine role essential to what he considered the gracious society in Chessie's increasing aggressiveness, and if he might not enjoy the idea of bringing out the woman behind the Vestal in Anita. Why should anyone have to assume that he would be as clumsy as the great Emily's preceptor?

It was only a few days after the evening at *Siegfried* that Anita came to his office with a countenance of deep concern.

"Miss Speddon wants to talk to you. She asks you to forgive her for not coming to the museum, but she has not been at all well."

"But of course!" he exclaimed, jumping up. "Shall I go to her now?"

"Well, I wouldn't delay it too long. I think she wants to discuss her will." She paused and then, in what struck him as an overdramatic gesture, clasped her hands beseechingly. "Oh, Mark, *do* be careful! I know you have very definite ideas about how she should leave her things. But please, please remember, that collection has been her whole life!"

He found that he was actually trembling with the sudden shock of his indignation. "And what do you think I plan to do with the collection? Hock it all and buy wrecked automobiles or old toilet seats or whatever modern art is featuring when she dies? Is *that* what you think of me?"

She recoiled as if he had moved to strike her. "No, no. It's not that at all. If *you* were the only judge, I'd have no worries. Believe me!"

"And how do you know I won't be?"

"Oh, Mark, if you only were."

Somewhat mollified, he settled back in his chair. "Trust me, Anita. Try to trust me."

"I will, I will. I want to so much."

After she had gone he reflected irritably that it must be a sense of guilt that had caused his fit of temper. Yet why should he feel guilty? Had he made any representation to Anita, either by word or implication, as to the state of his mind or affections that was not true? Had she not just admitted that she was aware of his belief that a museum should be the absolute owner of its own artifacts? And did she not know on just what terms he was with Chessie? Could a Puritan in the Massachusetts Bay Colony have been more open?

Yet he was still flustered when he called that afternoon at 36th Street. The very fact that Anita was still at the museum and that Miss Speddon was to see him alone intensified a silly feeling of conspiracy. The old lady received him upstairs in her bedroom. She was fully dressed but sitting in a wheelchair, and she seemed gaunter beside the huge canopied bed draped in red damask. She made no secret of the state of her health.

"A will seems more real when you think of your executors 'executing' it in a few months' time. Then it's more like a contract with an imminent closing date."

"That's the way to look at it, of course. You should think of a will as operating now."

"Very true, young man." There was a faint smile on those thick white lips. "But if 'now' is a time when you will be extinct, the idea can give you a turn."

"I am sure it must."

"You are trying to be sympathetic, and I should be grateful. But there's a dreadful gulf between the young living and the old dying. We latter sometimes even feel a silly kind of superiority. I must avoid that. To work!" She moved as if to square her long sloping shoulders. "I'm beginning to see your point about the futility of rigid rules for governing my things."

She paused to look at him carefully.

"One has to put one's trust in someone, I suppose," he offered, a bit weakly.

"That's well put," she replied judiciously. "I was afraid you'd say, 'Oh, you can trust the museum!' Which is of course what you meant. But a good administrator should not appear too eager. Yes, I like that, Mr. Addams."

He opted for a candid laugh. "You know too much about us, Miss Speddon. And please call me Mark."

"Very well, I will. Mark. Because I like you. And of course I don't trust the museum — the museum, that is, as it may become in the future. I used to tell Sidney Claverack's father, the old surrogate — he married my mother's cousin, you know — that I wanted him to tie up my collection so that it would take a wicked director, aided by a wicked board of trustees, a hundred years to unravel it. Oh, I knew they'd be able to do it in the end. I'm not an idiot. I've read about what happens to charitable trusts. The best way to do it, Judge Claverack used to tell me, was by a defeasance clause so that the family got everything back if the conditions were violated. In that way, he said, you'd always have an alert watchdog, not just some sleepy old bank or trust company. But families die out." She shook her head gravely before adding, "And some families can be bought."

Mark reflected that an apparent detachment seemed to be his most effective role. "You could name as taker in default another museum. Then you'd have a real watchdog!"

Again she seemed amused. "You really are a very clever young man. Yes, that would not be a bad idea at all. But museums, too, can be bought. And museums can merge."

"Aren't you perhaps overly concerned, Miss Speddon? Even the most aggressive museums today are not apt to forget the names of their patrons. Indeed, they seem the one thing they cherish. Look at the names preserved in everlasting marble in our city: Morgan, Frick, Guggenheim, Whitney —"

"Mark, Mark, hush up!" She held up both hands to check him. "Don't undo your good work. It's not my silly name I care about. Isn't there something ignoble about all those burghers and bankers hitching a ride to immortality on the shoulders of the artists they've bought? No, dear boy, I'm way beyond that."

Chastened, Mark was silent in the pause that followed.

"Judge Claverack taught me something of the wisdom of the common law," she continued, having recognized his subdual. "I learned that property could not be tied up in trust for longer than lives in being. *Lives* in being. Which meant a person or persons actually alive when the trust was set up. That was the limit beyond one's own death to which one should properly look. Of course, I know that charitable trusts can be set up in perpetuity, but as I have just indicated, I put no faith in perpetuity. So I have been considering that I should limit myself to the more reasonable restrictions of the common law. Lives of persons I know, Mark. Of course most of them are old, like myself."

"But you must have many young friends, Miss Speddon. You have been the patroness of so many young artists."

"Yes. But there is one young person who is more than a friend. Whom indeed I love like a daughter. Unless granddaughter be the more appropriate term."

He hesitated. "Anita?"

"Anita. Of course. Nobody knows my things the way she does. And nobody cares more."

He elected to be generous. "That is very true."

"So long as she has a role in the management of my collection, I shall have a kind of posthumous existence. But I learned something else from Sidney's father about what lawyers call 'perpetuities.' Those lives in being were at one time reduced to two. Two lives in being was the limit! Well, I have decided, Mark, that two is enough for me."

"You mean you would suspend the museum's absolute ownership of what you leave to it for the duration of two lives?"

"Not legally, perhaps. Let us say morally. I haven't worked it out with the lawyers yet. But can you guess whose the second life would be?"

He bit his lip and took the chance. "Not mine, surely?"

"Yours."

He jumped up and strode to the middle of the room. What could she possibly mean? That he and Anita should be her trustees?

"I'm sorry, Miss Speddon. I don't understand. I sense that you're offering me a great compliment, perhaps a great trust, but I don't see how it's meant to work."

"Sit down, my friend. Sit down and listen to me." She waited while he complied. "I'm going to talk to you with what may strike you as a shocking candor. But I claim the privilege of the moribund. Pray do not interrupt until I have finished." She folded her thin, brown, speckled, blue-veined hands in her lap and gazed down at them. "I sense you have a more than casual interest in Anita, and I suspect she has at least an equal one in you. Oh, I'm quite aware that nothing may come of this. I'm not a romantic old fool. And I also know you have some kind of attachment to a young woman in Sidney's office, though I'm told this may be on the wane. There is certainly no impediment on Anita's side. I intend to leave Anita a bequest that will make her, if not rich, at least independent for life. I think you should know this, not because I deem you mercenary, but on the contrary because I deem you not in the least mercenary. You have voluntarily adopted a profession that will yield you a small fraction of the income that a man of your abilities could command on today's financial market. I know this from Sidney, who has the highest regard for you. Indeed, he assures me that you have his voice for the directorship of the museum. If you and Anita should ever see your way to marrying, you would have a comfortable income between you."

Mark was almost panting now. There was simply too much to take in. "And your collection? How would it be affected?"

"I am relieved that you do not reject the idea of matrimony out of hand."

"Oh, no. Oh, no. Not at all."

"Good. That is more than a start. Very well. Here it is. I exact no hard conditions. If Anita can tell me there is no obstacle to your union, that you and she can contemplate with equanimity the probability — no, I do not even stipulate that — the *possibility* that your relationship may one day develop into marriage, I will bequeath my collection and two thirds of my residuary estate outright, unconditionally, to the museum."

"But, Miss Speddon, think of all the chances you'd be taking! I might die, or Anita might change her mind, or the museum might fire me . . . Anything could happen."

"I am fully aware of all that. I am also aware that I have very little time. The will must be drawn and signed. I am quite willing to take the chance that you and Anita may decide just to be friends. You would still be united in taking care of my things at the museum. Perhaps even more united. Moral obligations can be stronger than legal ones. Aren't gambling debts paid first for the very reason that they can't be enforced at law? Oh, you needn't worry about me, my lad. I'm an old Machiavelli!"

Mark made no apology now for rising and pacing the long chamber. His mind was astonishingly clear. He guessed that Sidney had been the one to tell Miss Speddon of the deterioration of his relations with Chessie. How had he known? At the office, of course. They always knew everything at the office. And wasn't it perfectly true? At least on his part? Hadn't Chessie been riding him unmercifully? And wasn't the prospect of Anita's submissive passion at least as agreeable as Chessie's hard green stare? Not to speak of Anita's future income being easier to live with than Chessie's future partnership percentage? For wouldn't he and Anita both owe their affluence to Miss Speddon, as opposed to his being constantly reminded of Chessie's greater earning power? And he would be director! Oh bliss, oh tenfold bliss, oh bliss ineffable and unimaginable! He felt a fierce, painful swelling about his heart. What normal man would not be tempted by so noble and inspired an offer?

He turned to the old lady and exclaimed, "Miss Speddon, I will say just what you want me to say!"

"No more?"

He paused. It was important with her not to overdo it. Never to overdo it.

"No more. But I will say it happily. I will say it enthusiastically."

"Then that's all I ask. Let us seal our bargain with a handshake, dear boy. And tell Anita to speak to me when you and she are ready."

6

WHEN MARK went to Chessie's apartment after work he had still not spoken to Anita. He thought he might be able to gain some insight from Chessie about the proposed revision of her client's will. But it turned out to be an unfortunate topic.

Chessie's apartment reflected her personal philosophy in being starkly free of frills. The furniture, of black metal and canvas, was minimal, and there were two wall-sized abstracts, fields of single color, a black on black and a red on red. Over the logless fireplace hung a nude portrait of her late brother.

"You mean you've been sweet-talking the old girl out of her last penny and bibelot" was her sour comment. "Really, you curators are the limit! And you have the nerve to talk about lawyers. Is there a single brassiere or pair of panties you haven't wheedled out of the poor creature?"

"I'm only doing what your boss told me to do," he retorted hotly. "I'm following the advice of your sacred firm."

"Why? You're not its bond slave like me. What's the point

of being an unpaid prostitute? In your shoes I'd at least claim the luxury of independence from Claverack."

"Even if he could make you director of the museum?"

"What's the point of being that if you're still at his beck and call? At least if I get to be his partner I'll have a voice in the running of his firm. But it looks to me as if he'll have you so tied up, you won't be able to call your soul your own. If you still have a soul at that point."

"Is that so? Well, you may find that Sidney Claverack's director is quite as independent as his law partner. Particularly if he has Miss Speddon's spiritual heir behind him!"

"Oh, so that's it. I *see*. We are counting on Miss Vogel, are we? No wonder you've been so assiduous in your attentions recently. Did I compare you two to Higginson and Emily Dickinson? Forgive me for the wrong literary reference. I should have looked to Henry James. It's *The Aspern Papers*, isn't it? You get the treasure if you marry the old girl's niece. Except it's not the niece but the companion, the dim, rather faded companion. No doubt she will perk up — or even blossom — when she hears the hot vows of her passionate if slightly mercenary director."

"Chessie, you're absolutely impossible!" He rose and put down his unfinished drink. "And if you think for a minute I'm going out to dinner with you after that —"

"Heavens, no! Call Miss Vogel. No doubt she's crouching by the phone, waiting for the sound of her master's voice. But we don't like the word 'master,' do we? It reminds us unpleasantly of degrees we don't have. Very well, her B.A.'s voice."

Mark left the apartment without deigning to reply. In a booth at the corner drug store he telephoned Miss Speddon's house. "Are you free for dinner?" he asked abruptly when he got Anita. "I've something important to discuss. It's about Miss Speddon."

"They're just about to bring me something on a tray."

"Tell them to freeze it. Meet me at Leon's at Fifty-third and Third. Twenty minutes?"

He took her startled silence for assent and hung up.

At the restaurant, waiting for Anita, he drank off first one and then another large Martini. As soon as he felt the humming calm in his head from the rapid dosage, he tried to focus his attention on the problem of being honest with himself. He liked to think that he always at least tried to be this, but for half a dozen hours now he had been living in a state of near euphoria.

To begin with, he asked himself, would a man in love find it necessary to brace himself with two strong drinks while waiting for the object of his affections? No. Certainly not.

But did this have to imply an aversion to poor Anita? A dread of intimacy? The possibility of impotence in the marriage bed, supposing it were to come to that? No. The only thing that really bothered him about Anita as a woman was her intensity. If she could be drunk or drugged, he could imagine her slim body as something pleasant to possess. He liked to imagine her submitting to him in spite of herself, giving in to an uncontrollable body urge, rather than to a noble and lofty passion that sought its excuse in one that matched it.

Was he then simply apprehensive that she would despise him if she were to suspect his motives? That she could never hope to love on such a basis? Yes. Which had to mean, didn't it, that he really despised those motives himself? And yet why should he? Had not millions of males married in part for personal advantage? Had it not been the rule rather than the exception throughout recorded history that dower should rank romance? Was "love, love, love" not recognized the world over as a uniquely American phenomenon, and not always taken seriously even there? What was the point of lashing one's back for what everyone else felt and did?

What he really wanted, he supposed in a burst of candor with himself, was an Anita who would come to him out of simple duty, an Oriental bride with downcast eyes, delivered by her father, with the dowry of a herd of oxen, to the vigorous embraces of a stranger which she would find unexpectedly delightful. That was it! If he and Anita were only expected to screw for the museum, screw for Miss Speddon's collection, they might be wonderfully paired! Why did life have to be unnecessarily complicated?

And there she was, moving quickly towards him between the tables, in her unmistakeable self-deprecatory way, yet with a kind of self-possession, too, as if, in apologizing for brushing against the back of someone's chair, she nonetheless insisted on the necessity of her doing so because she was on a mission from someone whose command was absolute. Their eyes met, and she offered him a stiff little smile.

As she slipped into the chair opposite, she glanced at his empty glass. "I'm glad you haven't waited for me."

"Oh, I've had a couple," he replied with affected ease. He hailed the waiter and ordered two more. "Frankly, I wanted the start on you because I've got something rather difficult to say. I had a talk with Miss Speddon this morning. She told me about her heart."

"Of course, you had to know," she said in a low voice, unfolding her napkin.

"There's something very much on her mind. Something she's anxious to have cleared up before she goes."

She looked up sharply. "And what is that?"

"She's got it into her head that you and I should get married. And she'd like to have some assurance of this before she dies."

"Oh dear, I was afraid she was going to say something like that."

Mark was astonished at her tone. Was it possible that the old girl had taken her into her confidence? "Is the idea so repulsive to you?"

"I don't think I have to answer that. Any relationship between you and me would be a matter quite independent of what Miss Speddon thought or wished."

"Is that really so? When she cares so much? And when she may be dying?"

He noted the flicker of pain across her brow. "What are you getting at, Mark?"

"Well, would it be a mortal sin if you were to tell her that, yes, something might be going to happen between you and me? She hates the idea of leaving you alone in the world. She feels that she's helped herself to great slices of your life —"

"It's not true! It's not true!" Suddenly she was almost sobbing.

He decided to wait for the drinks before going on. When they came, he observed how eagerly she reached for hers. He began to feel on surer ground.

"It doesn't really matter whether it's true or not," he went on now. "What matters is the peace and security that you could so easily give her in her last weeks or months."

Her suspicion was now tinted with something close to hostility. "Why are you suddenly taking such a great interest in Miss Speddon's peace of mind?"

"Because she's the patron saint of the museum I love!" he rang out roundly. Oh, he had the right note now! "Because we owe her so much and are going to owe her more. Because she's the greatest collector of Americana in the country. And because I've come to be devoted to her. I didn't hesitate to tell her what she wanted to hear from me!"

"What was that?" She looked almost scared.

"Why, that I was willing to marry you, of course. There is no point doing things halfway."

"You had no objection to telling her a bare-faced lie?"

"A lie? Who's to say it's a lie? Who knows what might develop between you and me in the future? Why should I make a dying woman miserable by telling her that something is never going to happen that for all I know, and for all *you* know, could happen?"

"I thought you had other commitments."

"I have no commitments, Anita. I told Miss Speddon that, and it's true. Chessie Norton and I are not engaged."

"Well, maybe not engaged exactly . . ."

"We've been lovers, if that's what you mean. Have you never had a lover?"

"Actually, I have."

He tried not to show his surprise. He even found a moment to wonder whether he might not actually be jealous. The wretched Sweeters must have got further than he had supposed. "Well, then there is no reason that we should not be sophisticated and realistic in such matters."

"I think there are lots of reasons."

"But none that should keep you from giving poor Miss Speddon the reassurance she needs."

"Why must she have it from me when she's already had it from you?"

"Because she told me so."

She gaped. "She did?"

"Of course she did. Do you think she takes it for granted that you'd have me?"

"Yes!"

At this she covered her face with both hands and remained silent for so long that he was uneasily aware that people were beginning to stare.

"Please, Anita."

"Mark, I want to go home. I don't want any dinner."

"Oh, surely now . . ."

"If I'm going to think about this at all I've got to be alone." She turned to the waiter, who was approaching with the menu cards. "Will you bring us the check, please? I'm afraid we can't stay. I'm not feeling well."

In the taxi, while she sat huddled in a corner, staring out the window, he felt the elation of the last cocktail, which had been a double. It had worked out almost too well. For he was convinced that she would be unable to withhold from her beloved mistress this final consolation, and he was also persuaded that Miss Speddon would not tell Anita about the will change. She would know that Anita would be opposed to it and would dread the weariness of the argument necessarily entailed. He would have gained what he wanted without the risk of Anita's counter-arguments. And without committing himself to Anita!

And then, as if he had fallen out of the suddenly opened door of the cab and struck his head on the sidewalk, the blow of depression fell. How could he, nice Mark Addams, be such an utter shit?

"Anita," he murmured, reaching for her hand, "Anita, listen to me. You mustn't think I have no feeling about all this. I meant that about the future. Who *is* to tell what might happen between you and me?"

"Oh, Mark, shut up, please."

"I mean it!"

"Just because you've had too many cocktails."

"And what did you mean when you said that you knew Miss Speddon took for granted you'd have me? Why?"

"Never mind!"

"It's because you do care about me, isn't it?"

Reaching over now, he took her firmly by the shoulders and pressed his lips to hers. She resisted fiercely, but only for a moment before she returned his kiss with ardor. Then suddenly she broke roughly away. The cab had pulled up before Miss Speddon's house, and she was out of it and gone without a word.

7

MARK did not have to face repercussions from the little scene in the taxi, for the very next day Miss Speddon suffered another heart attack, and Anita did not reappear at the museum for the remaining three weeks of the old lady's life. Although the latter retained her mental faculties to the end, as evidenced by the new will that she executed, her younger companion felt she had to be constantly available to supervise the household and check on the nurses. And when she did return to her office, the day after the crowded funeral, where she had sat like a wraith in the front pew with Miss Speddon's nephew and niece, her demeanor did not invite any reference to osculation in cabs. She seemed a new presence, even soberer and more silent than before, yet possessed of a new air of confidence, a confidence, it seemed, not so much in herself as in the representative of the now divine deceased. She even addressed Mark as "Mr. Addams"!

But he had little difficulty in persuading himself that this was for the best. His life had suddenly exploded into a success so dazzling that he was going to need all his energies just to keep his balance. The role of women, Chessie as well as Anita, could be suspended for a time. Miss Speddon's will, which named Claverack executor and bequeathed her "chattels" and two thirds of her fortune outright to the museum, had been admitted to probate without contest, and shortly thereafter the chairman had summoned his trustees to executive session and informed them of the role Mark had played in persuading the testatrix to place such confidence in their institution. He had then asked and received their assent to Mark's appointment as permanent director.

The golden sky of Mark's new happiness, however, like most such celestial canopies, had a few intrusive clouds. He and Chessie had ceased to see each other since the night of their quarrel about Anita, but her legal duties to the Speddon estate brought her on occasion to the museum, and now she loomed in his doorway to raise her right arm in a mock salute.

"Hail to thee, Macbeth!"

"Which witch are you?"

"The one that gave Banquo the better news."

"You agree with him that I played 'most foully' for it?"

She made a pincers movement with her forefinger and thumb. "Not foully. Just a teensy weensy bit unethically. Nothing, really, in the world we live in."

Mark reddened. "I presume Miss Speddon's honorable counsel would not have sanctioned the will had there been any funny business."

"Oh, that's true enough. I'm not talking about anything as ugly as 'undue influence.' But there are degrees in what I at least consider permissible persuasion. A testator of sound mind can still be bamboozled a bit."

"And you are suggesting that I bamboozled Miss Speddon?"

"Let's put it that you can be very charming, Mark. When you want to be."

"And let's put it that now is not one of those times."

It was simple enough to turn his back on Chessie, for she was never one to thrust her presence on a man, but he found it harder to know how to comport himself with Anita, who treated him with the reserve of a competent lieutenant who has neither sought nor enjoyed the friendship of the commanding officer.

What had happened behind that passive brow? For Mark knew that she was far too tense to have escaped all inner turmoil. Sometimes he surmised that she had been overcome by a violent feeling of guilt at having allowed what should have been the white sheet of a total preoccupation with her mistress's dying agony to be stained with carnal thoughts. Was she not just the type of puritan who would condemn herself for these? But at other times, particularly when he fancied he could detect a glimmer of contempt in the steady gaze of her eyes at staff meetings, he wondered whether she had not scented a bargain between the terms of the new will and his amorousness in the taxi. If so, she must have branded him as an unscrupulous adventurer.

Well, was he not? Would he hesitate to do it over? Was he not now in a position to raise his museum to the heights of which the poets sing? Until today he felt he had been only half alive; *here* was the role for which he had been pining. He could reach out eager arms to take from the Isolde of his boyish fantasies the goblet that she offered, happy to quaff it whether it should prove death or passion so long as his heart might beat to the crash of a Wagnerian sea. His enthusiasm would have to prove contagious to all but the oldest of the old guard; his happiness would guarantee his good will, and his good will would be irresistible! Even Anita would be obliged to admit he had acted in the best interests of her patroness, unless she was totally blinded by prejudice.

For the possibilities of the museum were now limitless. So wide was the area of its coverage, so vast its collections, that with the Speddon money it could choose any role in the cultural world it desired. It had been the beneficiary of the migration of wealthy New Yorkers from mansions to brownstones, and from brownstones to apartments, and from these to the suburbs, each step necessitating the shedding of quantities of furniture, porcelain, silver, gold, clothes and even jewelry. Why, the museum had trunks in its warehouse that had never been opened! He would now unite the staff in the task of overhauling, recataloguing and redisplaying the collections. The institution, once faded and shabby, the darling of old maids and widows, now, like the somnolent court in *The Sleeping Beauty,* would awaken to glitter and dance. Even the impassive guards would be aware that a new spirit had invaded the land.

But Anita's presence persisted. There came an interview with her that made Mark feel the deflation of the Hans Christian Andersen milkmaid who, daydreaming on her way to market of the riches that the pail balanced on her pate would bring once its contents had been sold and magically reinvested, tossed her head with the vain gesture of the princess she would then be and spilled the milk.

"I trust it is not too early to ask the director what steps the administration is contemplating to ensure the proper housing of Miss Speddon's collection."

He found her tone distinctly abrasive. "What housing?"

"Well, surely you don't think Miss Speddon's things can be accommodated in our present space?"

" 'Our' space? I see. This old dog of an institution is going to have to get used to being wagged by its new tail. And just how do you suggest that we inflate our present quarters?"

"Don't we — excuse me, 'you' — own the vacant lot to the west? And the two brownstones beyond that? You have room to put up a large annex."

"An annex! With building costs what they are? You dream, Miss Vogel."

"I do not dream, Mr. Addams. Miss Speddon has left the museum millions. Far more than is needed to care for all of her things. Of course it was her intention that they should be properly housed, and of course she expected to pay for it."

Mark stared. This *was* a new Anita. He wondered whether even Chessie would not change her mind if she heard her now. "But that money is for endowment. We never promised Miss Speddon that we would build with it."

"Cannot promises be implied? From all the acts and dealings of the parties? I suggest you ask Miss Norton about that."

Mark could think of nothing to say to this, but the subject was still very much on his mind at his weekly conference with the chairman of the board. He asked Sidney if there had been any understanding with Miss Speddon about increasing the size of the museum.

"Increasing it? What the hell for?"

"To take care of all her artifacts. Miss Vogel seems to think that's what you were to use the money for."

"Miss Vogel thinks *I* am going to use good endowment money to put a roof over all that junk? Miss Vogel is a greater fool than I took her for."

Sidney Claverack, Mark supposed, used the personal pronoun both in his capacity as museum chairman and as executor of the will. He evidently regarded himself in fact as well as in law as the living embodiment of the late Evelyn Speddon.

"Junk!" Mark murmured, glancing at the door. Fortunately it was closed.

"Well, not all of it, of course. I'll have to do a lot of winnowing out. But when we've picked out the pearls, I think you'll find they'll all fit easily into our present space."

"And the rest?"

"Well, what the hell do you think, Mark? The rest will be sold, of course."

What really appalled Mark was the sudden, illuminating realization that he was more appalled than surprised. The veil through which he had long contemplated the chairman could have been of no one's devising but his own.

"Miss Vogel, I suppose, will expect to have something to say about that."

"That spook of a girl? Surely, Mark, you don't think a mere amanuensis of our late benefactress is going to stand in the way of institutional progress?"

"You may be underestimating her, sir. She can be very strong when she's defending the Speddon collection."

"And she can also be fired." Sidney seemed to find it irksome that such a fly should have the temerity to alight even momentarily on him. He waved his hand as if to dispose of Anita. "I know all about Miss Vogel. It's my job as a lawyer to know these things. Other than a small trust fund which reverts, anyway, to the museum at her death, Miss Vogel has no legal interest whatever in the Speddon estate or in the collection. Even her job here is totally in our discretion. She had better learn prudence if she wants to stick around this place."

"But she might raise some kind of a stink."

"My dear boy, she's a nobody! I don't know what's got into you today. It's not like Mark Addams to fuss like this. If you're really worried about her, I'm sure a minimum of attention on your part would settle her hash. I've seen the way she stares at you. Oh, yes, I notice these things! Give her the good old limey slap and tickle, and she'll shut her silly mouth."

Mark could not help bursting into laughter at so remarkable a misconstruction of Anita's character, and his mirth helped to quell his doubts. But not altogether. "Of course it was you, Sidney, who induced me to persuade Miss Speddon to make the terms of her will less rigorous. Doesn't that impose on me some kind of a moral responsibility to see that her intentions are carried out?"

"You may carry out your moral obligations any way you see fit. But you are still subject to the wishes of the trustees. Don't ever forget that, my boy. And the sole moral obligation of the trustees is to do what is best for the institution they serve. So you can be, in the immortal phrase of our almost impeached president, as 'candy ass' as you choose. It is not going to make a particle of difference to any of us."

"You mean the board won't care about the intentions of Miss Speddon?"

"My dear fellow, you are being positively crude. Of course the board will care. The board will care very much. But it has always been my firm tenet that the intentions of a decedent, expressed or implied, legally binding or merely morally so, must be construed, like our revered Constitution, in accordance with changing times and conditions. The one thing we can never know is what a dead person would have thought about any current issue if alive. And for that simple reason it is necessary for the dead to rely on the living to decide these questions. It isn't a matter of should or should not. There is simply no way that the dead can choose."

"But aren't you speaking of the passage of considerable time? Surely it can't be that difficult to interpret intentions expressed only months ago?"

And now Mark saw for the first time in his own experience — though he had certainly heard about it from others — the shadow that flitted across the features of the chairman when he found himself confronted with that rare individual who did not know how to bend before the right persuasion.

"I think you may be forgetting, Mr. Director, that I am looking forward to our working together congenially in the years to come. Obviously you and I do not wish anything to change our happy relationship."

Mark swallowed hard. "Nothing will, sir, of course."

Sidney rose to his feet, at once beaming, and turned to the door. "That is just fine, fella. Just fine. But just don't you forget it."

If Anita Vogel had been associated with his initial rise to power at the museum, he supposed it was only fair that the first crack in the smooth surface of his professional success should coincide with the rift in the sympathy between them.

If the cheerful countenance of Sidney Claverack was now overcast with a hint of admonition, with the unpleasant reminder that future benefits were not going to be accorded without some contribution by the beneficiary, might it not have been anticipated that the woman on whose affections he had based his plan of advance should be at least in part the cause?

She burst into his office, pale with anger, the very next morning, to ask if he knew that the executors of Miss Speddon's estate had already disposed of her doll collection at a private sale. And he hadn't! And then a very peculiar thing took place, something he could not explain at the time or afterwards. He had been standing by the window of his office when she came in, and she had gone up to him, pressing her irate face closely, almost menacingly, to his. Certainly there was nothing in the least like a sexual advance in her attitude; on the contrary, it seemed to fling his old fantasies to the scrap heap of vulgar things with which a Vestal Virgin could have nothing to do. There was something in her white, desperate stare that appeared to slam the ivory gates of the world of art and beauty and relegate him to the lesser kingdom of Claverack, in which he was doomed to play a minor and even a humiliating role. And it might have seemed his last chance or at least his own final gesture of defiance to kiss her suddenly on her wet lips.

"Mr. Addams, you have insulted me!" she cried in a hoarse voice, jumping back and placing a chair between them. "I see now I was a fool to imagine you could ever be a friend or that you could ever care about anything but crowds and headlines. Well, there may be one soul in this jungle of philistines who will listen to me! I'll take my case to Mr. Hewlett. We'll see if *he* will allow the museum to be plundered by you and your crooked shyster of a boss!"

And before he could say another word, she was gone.

8

PETER HEWLETT was always the first down for breakfast, and although Ida, the waitress, had set the table the night before and was ready in the pantry, having lit the fire, for his ring, it was a ritual, on dark winter mornings, for the lights to be left off so that the master himself might turn the switch. He loved the moment when, after a brief flickering, the bulbs over the paintings suddenly flashed on bright, and the room would be filled with their dazzling colors: the voluptuous blues and yellows of Manet's *Venetian Canal with Gondola,* the green and dusty effulgent reds of Gauguin's island goddess and the grays and yellows of Van Gogh's bartender in Arles, whose thick curly gray hair and mustache, whose humped shoulders and pale worried limpid eyes, were uncannily like Peter's own reflection in the mirror over the sideboard with the guardian eagles on its cornices. A collector's life was made up of such moments.

Peter went to the bay window and gazed out at the gray beach beyond the lawn and the slatey stretch of Long Island

Sound. He loved the dreary blackness of early winter and the gleam of the silver coffee urn before the crackle of the small fire in the grate. Then he noted that the Whistler Venetian etching was slightly ajar and he adjusted it carefully. The sudden sound of a bell somewhere in the house put him in mind of his alarm system, though of course it was not that. Augusta was simply ringing for her maid. But did the alarm system really work? There had been that terrible business at the Covingtons', just down the road, the winter before. Someone, bold as brass, had parked a van before the front door and carted half their treasures away! But then they had been off in Europe without even a caretaker left in the house. What did such feckless people expect? Peter had, in addition to his alarm system, a couple permanently in the house and an outside watchman when he and Augusta were in town, and, of course, the maids in addition on weekends, as now.

Yet what could maids really do? And the night watchman, mightn't he doze off? Or be bound and gagged? Or bribed? Yes, even in the apartment on Park Avenue, with all the men in the lobby and on the elevators, how could you guard against a clever burglar who might offer a Puerto Rican at the service entrance ten thousand dollars in *cash* to let him up? Why not? Wouldn't it be worth more than that to steal a Renoir, not to speak of Augusta's diamond earrings? Oh, the jewelry, to hell with that — it was insured, anyway — but the pictures, my God, the pictures!

Peter had rung now for his breakfast, and he tried to distract himself by greeting Ida cheerfully and watching her as she poured his coffee. He knew his moments of nervous seizure were always going to come and go — they always had — and that he must concentrate on the good moments, which were very good indeed. How many men were blessed at sixty-nine with health and wealth, a loving wife and a great collection? Was it his sin to have loved the pictures too much? But then was there any point, after the passage of almost the biblically allotted life span, to pretend he was anything he wasn't?

He brought the cup to his lips and drank too quickly, scalding his tongue. Fire! Oh, my God, fire! The apartment where three quarters of the collection was kept was moderately safe, but this long white structure that Augusta had refused to build of stone, this rambling two-story villa so charmingly adapted to the garden and lawns around it and to the ivy that crept over the columns of the verandas, would it not explode into a ball of flame before the pictures could be removed? There were sprinkling outlets in every room, fire extinguishers in every corridor, and each new member of the local fire brigade was invited to cocktails and instructed about the treasures — for hose water could be as damaging as the worst blaze — but what was all of this against the fury of a real conflagration? *Peter*, he warned himself, as he felt his heartbeat dangerously quicken, remember: each minute of life is to be lived *in* that minute. And there is no fire now. Enjoy your pictures *now*.

He breathed more easily. He had not really burned his tongue after all. Ida had gone out to the pantry and was coming back with his poached eggs and bacon. He never tired of poached eggs and bacon. And here was Augusta, serene and understanding, with her lovely pale gray skin and hair, and sapphire eyes which still managed to be mild, and those wonderful big pearls on her ear lobes and a sweater that matched them. Why had she married him, this rare creature, who at fifty-five could have passed for ten years younger?

"Good morning, my darling wife."

"Good morning, my dear."

"Seeing you revives me. I was thinking of fire again."

"What a silly thought. You know the house is as safe as we can make it."

"Except we could always move the best pictures to the apartment."

"And not have them here where we enjoy them and where we live almost half the year? You know you'd hate that. Just remember, my dear, they're a good deal safer than they ever were with their former owners, in France or wherever. Probably in some old château with no air conditioning or firefighting equipment. You've done more than your duty by them."

Ah, she always said the right thing! When she wanted to, anyway. But then, immediately, he felt the need to pull her down a bit, perhaps because he depended on her so much.

"Why is the table set for five?" he demanded. "Who besides ourselves and Inez and Julia are expected? You know, Gussie, I will *not* have children at the breakfast table. Breakfast should be a quiet meal."

"Inez promised Carter he would graduate from the children's table when he was twelve."

"But he won't be twelve until next month!"

"Really, Peter, must we be so technical?"

"Yes! When it comes to a question of noisy breakfasts. I shall not abrogate the rule a day before the prescribed limit. Ida, will you please move Carter's plate to the conservatory." And he added in a lower voice while Ida was carrying this out, "Give Inez an inch, and you know what she'll take!"

Inez Eliot, the oldest of the three Hewlett daughters, had been abandoned by her husband, a TV anchorman in Memphis, for an eighteen-year-old girl and had come resentfully home with her brood of five. It had been agreed that she would live in the Long Island house, which her parents occupied only on weekends, until she had found something of her own, and Peter had at first relished the prospect of the big place resounding once more with the sound of children, but as the indolent Inez seemed to find herself thoroughly comfortable and well waited on, the arrangement now threatened to become permanent.

Her presence, large and what her father distastefully deemed "dumpy" or even "doughy"—he could not quite help a concealed sympathy for his errant son-in-law — crowned by an Iberian blackness of hair and brow, followed hard upon the waitress's removal of her son's service. Peter used to wonder if naming her for Augusta's Spanish grandmother had not affected her looks.

"I thought, Mummie, that Carter would be eating with us."

Inez's small, red-haired, freckled boy appeared suddenly from behind his parent. "It's all right, Mom. I'd rather be with the others. But tell me first, Grandpa, is that a Manet? Our new art teacher said yesterday you own one of the great Manets."

"All Manets are great," replied Peter, already regretting the boy's banishment. "And, yes, that is indeed a Manet. Do you like it? I daresay you think you could draw a more realistic-looking gondola."

The boy squinted for a moment at the Venetian study and then shook his head. "Nobody could paint a better gondola than that."

Peter grunted with pleasure as the boy ran off into the conservatory. "That lad may grow up to be a collector."

"Carter has a painter's eye," Augusta agreed.

"I don't know where he'd get the money to buy paintings," Inez grumbled. "And anyway, if that's the case, I'd rather he'd be a painter and not just a collector."

" 'Just' a collector, Inez?"

"Well, it's not belittling collectors, is it, Daddy, to put painters ahead of them?"

"It most certainly is. And your remark was obviously designed to put me in my place."

"Oh, Dad, you're so prickly. Surely even you will admit that collecting is not as creative as painting or sculpting."

"I will admit no such thing! Where would Italian art be without the great patrons of the Renaissance? Who would have supported Raphael or Michelangelo had there been no collecting popes?"

"We know all that. But today you don't need patrons. And if

you did, they'd be a dime a dozen. Every millionaire from here to Tokyo collects impressionists."

"I suppose it's too much to expect that one's own children should try to understand what one has spent one's lifetime trying to accomplish," Peter said bitterly. "But I still wish to instruct you, Inez, that my collection is not simply a medley of European canvases. It is a carefully selected assemblage of those European and Asiatic paintings and drawings that have given rise to the greatest number of what I call American counterparts. And I have attempted to match these with the works of Americans executed under their influence so that my collection will give a sense of the glory of the inspiration and the glory of the result!"

But Inez was quite as determined not to be impressed as he was to impress her. "Surely you don't need that many pictures to make the simple point that American artists were influenced by foreigners."

"But I do! To make my point not simply but magnificently."

"And how do you make it with the pictures locked up here or in the apartment?"

"You know they're always available to students," Peter retorted in exasperation. "Weren't you complaining only last week of the bus tour from Hunter College that interrupted your children's sacred lunch hour? And of course eventually they'll all be together in a museum."

"All? You mean you're planning to leave your *whole* collection to charity?"

"Certainly I am. If by charity you mean the Museum of North America."

"Whoa! I knew you were leaving the American paintings there. And I suppose they belong there. But the European ones? The *great* paintings? Dad, that's a fortune!"

"You think they should go to your hungry kids, Inez?"

This last, in a clear, cool, yet not unfriendly tone, came from the doorway where Inez's sister Julia had just appeared. The only still unmarried, yet handsomest of the daughters, this tall, dark-haired Miss Hewlett had the soft features and shining blue eyes of her mother, somewhat hardened, or perhaps jelled, by the smart cut of her brown suit and maroon blouse, dressed as she was for the city and for a busy day at her decorating firm.

"I hardly think it's proper, girls," Augusta intervened, "that we should be discussing your father's will at the breakfast table. Or at any meal, for that matter."

"Well, if I'm going to be disinherited, I think I'd better know about it," Inez exclaimed, aggrieved. "It's all very well for you, Mummie — you have your own money. And for you, Julia — you have your business and no other mouths to feed. But I think those with families, like Doris and me, are entitled to know where we stand."

"Disinherited!" Peter cried irately. "You deserve to be disinherited for such an asinine statement. Who do you think supports you now? And where do you think your trust fund came from? If my collection were left to the family, there wouldn't be money enough in my estate to pay the death taxes. Most of that stuff is worth ten times what I paid for it. It only makes sense to put it in a museum."

"Peter, you mustn't get so excited," Augusta warned him. "Now I suggest we talk about something else."

"Wait a sec, Ma," Inez enjoined her. "With inflation what it is today, how can anyone be sure there'll be enough money left to go around? You and Dad have eight grandchildren now and probably more to come. Julia may still marry and have kids." But the glance that the fecund Inez cast at her sister seemed to place this in doubt. "Where would Dad have been without *his* inheritance, I'd like to know?"

"But I've told you, Inez," her father, furious at this last, almost shouted. "The taxes would eat up the estate!"

"Not if the pictures were sold. Then there'd be enough for the taxes *and* your family."

"The pictures sold!"

"Well, not all of them, of course. You could direct that certain ones be sold and others go to your children and the museum. What's wrong with that?"

"Oh, you would allow me to leave a few to the museum? That's very gracious of you, Inez. I suppose I should be duly grateful. Which ones could go to the museum, do you suppose? The Victorian academics? Are they cheap enough now? But no, they're coming back, aren't they?"

"Of course, Dad, if you're not going to be serious, there's no point discussing the matter."

Peter picked up his plate, fork and napkin, and rose.

"I shall finish my breakfast in the library," he announced stiffly. "Augusta, will you kindly ask Ida to bring me in another cup of coffee?"

At his desk it was all he could do to cut the toast under his eggs with his shaking hands. Sell his pictures! That was what one could expect from children after supporting them in luxury all their lives, after setting up trust funds for them, after wasting precious hours with tedious lawyers determining how to squeeze the most out of one's liquid assets for their benefit. And all the time what they wanted was simply one's lifeblood! He smote the desk with his fist. Where the hell was his coffee? He was about to yell for Ida when the door opened. But it was not Ida who brought him his cup, but Augusta herself.

"I think we're allowing ourselves to get overwrought," she said soothingly. "Now drink your coffee while you and I discuss this matter calmly and rationally."

"I don't want to discuss it at all!"

"I know, dear. I didn't think it was the time, either, and I tried to stop Inez. But now the fat's in the fire, we may as well get on with it."

He stared at his impassive spouse. "Why must we discuss it at all?"

"Because despite her nastiness, there may be some sense in

what Inez says. Why don't we have an appraisal made of all the art and see where we stand?"

"My accountant takes care of that. You don't have to appraise things that go to charity. They're not part of the taxable estate."

"But, darling, you're begging the question. Let's find out just what we have before we plan what to do with it. There must be a dozen different ways of dividing your estate sensibly between your family and the museum."

"But, Augusta," he implored her, in despair at the prospect of losing his greatest ally, "satisfactory to whom? You seem to forget that I bought all the art I own, and most of it out of income, or capital gains, at prices that are a fraction of its present worth. If I leave the children the principal I inherited from my father, haven't I satisfied the most rigorous moral laws of family succession?"

"You seem to forget that I have a voice in this, dear. I've not been altogether a passive partner in your collecting, have I?" She paused to await the nod he could not rightfully withhold. It had been she, after all, who had pushed him into the purchase of the El Greco *Auto-da-fé*, the star of the collection. "I am sure, once we have all the facts and figures, that we'll be able to work out something not too far from what you wish to accomplish. But first I must have those facts and figures."

He ventured a sour little smile, as if he might be teasing her. "And if I refuse? It *is* my estate, after all."

"If you refuse, my dear Peter . . ." His now awesome spouse paused again. She did not have to blink an eye or underline a single word. She spoke with the simplicity and friendliness of one instructing a difficult child. "If you refuse and I die before you, things will come off as you wish. But if I survive you, and in that respect you must consider the difference in our ages . . ."

"As well as my heart and the immortality of your family!" he exclaimed, still desperately hoping to make a joke of it.

"Yes, consider by all means those things," she pursued relentlessly. "I would have a right of election, would I not? To take against your will? Isn't that how the lawyers put it?"

"Augusta, you wouldn't!" he could barely gasp.

"I can assure you, my dear, that I should exercise every legal right I had to bring about what I considered a fair and just division of your estate."

"Do you know that Sidney Claverack suggested, when I signed my last will, that I should ask you to waive your right of election? And I refused. Refused indignantly!" Peter's voice soared to a new pitch of bitterness and self-pity. "I told him you'd never attack my will!"

"Nor would I, for my own benefit. Even if you cut me off without a penny. But I shouldn't hesitate to claim my legal share and give it to the children if I thought you had shortchanged them."

"Shortchanged them! They'll be rich, Augusta."

"In that case I shouldn't interfere. But rich is a relative term, my dear. I must insist on my right to define it as of the time your will is proved. And now, having said what I came to say, I shall leave you to finish your coffee. A disagreeable thing that has to be stated should be stated only once. The next move is yours."

Peter sat with Julia in the back of the maroon Cadillac limousine, en route to the city, pouring out his wrath at her mother's position. Julia, from childhood, had been by far his favorite. Doris, the youngest, who made an almost embarrassing show of filial devotion, came second; Inez trailed Doris, a poor third.

"What you should do, Dad," Julia said, when he came at last to a pause, "is take the matter into your own hands. The collection, after all, is yours. Mummie may have helped you, sure, but I can't see that that gives her any moral right to dispose of it. You've already done plenty for us girls. Why should you provide for an indefinite population explosion of descendants? Give what you want to the museum *now.* Then it won't be subject to Mummie's right of election when you die."

"And how do you think your mother will feel about *that*?"

"She won't care. All Mummie worries about is doing her duty. Once you've taken the choice out of her hands, she'll be quite reconciled. I've even heard her say that too much money would be bad for the grandchildren. She'd never go against your wishes unless you left her in a position where she had to decide between her family and the museum. Well, don't leave her in one."

Peter glanced inquiringly at this umpire of his marital life. Was she laughing at the antics of both her parents? Did Julia set herself up to scorn the curious money morality of the older generation, with its little fetishes about "earned" and "unearned" income and what should be considered "one's own" to dispose of and what had to be passed on down the family line? Did Julia, proud and independent as she was, regard greenbacks as simply greenbacks, gold as simply gold? Very likely. But wasn't that an integral part of her cool intelligence and her good, friendly, steady, reliable filial feeling? What a treasure she was! And what was she doing now but reaching behind the curtain of his pretenses and pulling out the naked little squealing ego that lurked there? "Why not acknowledge the babe?" she seemed to be asking. "He may be a fine boy, after all."

"Can you really be so sure about your mother?"

"I think so. She sees life in terms of what God is expecting of Augusta Hewlett. He can't expect her to choose if there's no choice. Going to law to fight your last will and testament would be a most distasteful business to her. She'd be glad to be freed of it."

"If I really believed that! Oh, what happiness! For you

know, Julia, it wouldn't ever be a question of stripping my family. No matter what I did, there'd always be enough to educate the grandchildren, even to set them up in life, and —"

"Dad, I know all that," Julia interrupted firmly. "Inez is simply hysterical about that noisy litter of hers. Do what you think is right with your own things and do it now."

He leaned over to give her a quick peck on the forehead and then changed the subject, chatting nervously about this and that, anything to avoid thoughts that might intrude upon the glorious license she had just given him.

He told the chauffeur to drop Julia off at her shop on Madison Avenue and then proceeded down to the Chrysler Building, where Sidney Claverack's law firm occupied a high story. The white wall of the senior partner's office, facing a three-window panorama of the boroughs of Queens and Brooklyn, formed a huge mat for a Rauschenberg study of yellow and tan wheels and cogs, a fantasy of a factory interior.

"I have several things to discuss with you, Sidney, but let's get this one out of the way first." Peter handed a piece of blue notepaper, heavily scrawled, to the expressionless lawyer. When the latter made no move to take it, he dropped it on the desk. "I received it yesterday. I gather you know who it's from."

"Oh, yes. We've all heard from Miss Vogel."

"And what do you plan to do about her?"

"I've done it. I've fired her."

Peter started. "Was that wise?"

"It was unavoidable. After the things she said, not only to Mark Addams, but to me, there could be no place for her in the museum. I didn't even allow her to unpack her desk. I told her to clear out and that we'd send her things later."

"But, Sidney, what are people going to say? Read my letter. This girl claims that you conned Daisy Speddon into signing a will that would let you junk her collection and keep the money she meant to maintain it."

Sidney jumped to his feet and shook his fist in the air. "I don't give a good god damn what people say! Miss Speddon, in the full possession of her faculties, gave me a wide discretion, and I intend to use it. And use it to make her the greatest benefactor in the history of the museum! Now we can have all those things we've been dreaming about. And that she *knew* we'd been dreaming about. The new Mayan gallery. The Indian hall. The great Modern America wing! Do you think I'm going to be stopped by the shrieks of one crazed female who wants the money used for the care and feeding of a million gewgaws put together by whimsy and sentimentality? Sure, a few people are going to grumble. Sure, we'll get some angry letters. Maybe some nasty newspaper articles. But in two years' time nobody is going to remember even who Miss Vogel is, and everybody will be singing the praises of the board of trustees that brought about the renaissance of a great museum!"

"Sidney, Sidney, you're going too fast." Peter shook his head reproachfully. "This is a matter for the board. It may even be a matter for a special meeting."

"Look here, Peter." Sidney had resumed his seat and now leaned towards his co-trustee, his chin thrust forward, his hands placed palm down on the blotter, with an air of grave and final appeal. "You and I *are* that board. Between us we're responsible for half the annual contributions. Nobody else could or even wants to run the place. So long as we stand together, we're an irresistible force!"

"It may be as you say. But I have a conscience, Sidney. I respected and liked Daisy Speddon."

"Then put up any tablet or statue in her memory that you want. Rename the place the Evelyn Speddon Institute. I'll go along. And while we're on the subject, let me tell you something else. Something we can do now if you'll come up with a million bucks. The Peter K. Hewlett Gallery of American Painters and Their Forerunners. We can build it on the lot to the west, where there's room for your whole collection. Of course, I don't want to use too much of the Speddon money on another trustee's things . . . that might look too bad . . . but —"

"And anyway I shouldn't need the Speddon money," Peter interrupted hastily. "No, no, I could do it all myself. Oh, my God!" He jumped to his feet now, as if the whole sudden dazzling vision had exploded to lift him up and up. Who was this monster sitting so placidly at his desk before the panorama of the two boroughs? "Get thee behind me, Satan!" he fairly screeched and then marveled as the room echoed with the strange rattle of his own laughter.

9

THE COILED JADE SERPENT covered the whole blotter on Carol Sweeters's desk. Its emerald-green body formed sixteen concentric circles of diminishing circumferences; its head, with black orbs of eyes and a round bulbous snout, filled the small central space, its chin resting on the edge of the innermost coil, so that it appeared to be staring balefully at the curator. It was presumably a "vision serpent," symbolizing a hallucination of the Mayas, who saw some of their gods as zoomorphs. But the vision serpent was usually bicephalic. Where was the other head? Not broken off, for Carol could see on the outer circumference, where the beast diminished into a tail, what appeared to be a rattle. Why had he not been more struck by this when he had examined it in Zürich?

A fake? Pre-Columbian art had always peculiarly attracted forgers. Carol had brooded over this piece for two hours now without moving from his desk. He knew he couldn't be fooled. He *knew* it. He ran his fingers lightly over the jade scales and felt the feathers on the outer layer. Vision serpents sometimes had small feathers. But of course a forger would know that.

He closed his eyes and tried to imagine blood dripping from a wound on his hand, his knee, his thigh, seeking the giddiness that a Maya would experience as his strength eroded with the loss of his life fluid. Then he blinked and glanced quickly back at the serpent. Yes! There *was* a gleam of something like red in those opaque orbs, a kind of ruddy glow that now died away. The vision serpent was summoned up in a state of mind affected by loss of blood. Oh, let people say he was crazy — say it, that is, if he were ever a fool enough to utter his thoughts — but he *knew* he could always feel out a true Mayan piece.

"May I have another look, sir?"

It was Fred Farr in the doorway, spookily skinny and cerebral, with red, stiff, curly hair, buck teeth and a drooping jaw, a scholar, too much so, Carol thought, Teutonic in his concern with minutiae. He had already expressed unwelcome doubts.

"Don't tell me it should have two heads," Carol muttered. "In this particular part of the Yucatán the vision serpent made do with one."

A ghost of a smile indicated that Farr recognized the joke. "I suppose a forger's trouble would be in simulating reverence. He's apt to show too much or too little."

"And which does this?"

"That's what I can't make out."

"Why should it show any?" Carol demanded.

"Well, isn't Mayan art largely of a religious nature? Those anthromorphs and zoomorphs are all gods and goddesses or at least creatures of the spirit world. The man who made them must have worked for priests."

"Does that have to mean that he believed all the crap he heard from the priests?"

Farr formed his lips into a circle of faint surprise. "One doesn't tend to think of doubt among the Mayas. Like other early civilizations, theirs seems to have been marked by extreme conformity."

"Seems? To whom? And even if it was, that doesn't mean the artists conformed. In their minds, I mean. Great artists never believe in anything but art."

"Really? Would you say that of the Middle Ages? Would you say it, for example, of the man who carved the figures on the north transept of Chartres?"

Carol, exasperated, jumped up. "Well, of course there are always going to be exceptions. I'll concede that a few stone-cutters and glassmakers in the hysteria of the twelfth century may have believed that Jesus was born of a virgin and could walk on water. But the greatest artists, never! Do you think for a minute that Michelangelo and Leonardo weren't laughing up their sleeves at their silly popes and bishops? That's exactly what sets them apart from ordinary mortals. While the idiots of the human species were feeding each other to lions or flames, or cutting off their own balls for the gratification of sadistic deities, it was the artist who stood aside, knowing it was all grist for his own glorious mill! And that is why, too, now that the churches have fallen into disuse, or given place to nutsy California evangelists, the museums have become the true temples. The new godless are beginning to glimpse the terrible and wonderful truth that there is nothing on earth to worship but art!"

"It's an interesting thesis. Perhaps you should write a book on it."

"Oh, go soak your head."

"Yes, sir." But Farr turned back in the doorway. "Actually, I think I'm going to agree with you about the snake."

"Of course you are."

Carol returned to his silent study of the coiled asp. Staring into the center of its rings, he tried mentally to drape them around his torso and then to tighten their grasp, to be crushed by a beast converted into a giant anaconda, which indeed perhaps it was, so that in becoming it, he would be it, and being it, be its creator, for the artist and his product had become indistinguishable. That sculptor had lived under a cloudless sky amid broad flat plains; he had climbed to the top of the pyramid temple to survey the green and yellow vegetation for miles and miles, and he would have come down to his atelier to put the heart of the country and his own heart into this curled-up apod. And he would have been happy, happy as a mortal could be!

Damn the telephone.

"Mr. Sweeters? The director would like to see you."

"Tell his high mightiness, good Miss Swayne, that I will come to him by and by."

He swore under his breath. Addams, like the beak-nosed warrior with the eagle headdress in the tablet leaning against the wall, could go slit his penis. What else was he good for? There may have been some sense, after all, in the bloodletting customs of the Mayas. Most administrators of any period were good for nothing but to shed their own blood, and if the populace chose to believe that this propitiated the gods, it may have been the best thing they could do. If they weren't shedding their own blood, they'd sure as hell be shedding someone else's.

Double-damn the telephone.

"Carol? It's Anita. Can you still talk to me? Or am I such anathema up there it'll cost you your job?"

"If our little Napoleon has tapped this wire, I hope he's listening in right now. Do you hear me, Addams? You're 'nothing but the composition of a knave, beggar, coward, pandar, and the son and heir of a mongrel bitch.' "

"Heavens. You don't suppose he's really listening?"

"If he is, you can tell him it's from *Lear*. Kent to Oswald. For I doubt he got beyond *Twelfth Night* in high school."

"Oh, Carol, it's good to hear that old tone again. I've missed you."

"If that is so, the ghost of a starved feline in the streets of Newport must be haunting you."

He heard the sharp intake of her breath.

"Of course I've thought about that. I wouldn't be I, would I, if I hadn't? But do you know, Carol, I've wondered if I didn't come down on you too hard about that incident. When I last saw my mother, she asked about you, and somehow she got it out of me about that cat. She told me I was a perfect idiot, that cats really could live off the streets in a city, that millions did —"

"Ah, but did *I* know that? Did I care? No, I think you're going to have to see me as the devil I am. I didn't think twice about what was going to happen to that cat."

"But if I'd *told* you it was going to starve, Carol, and you'd believed me, you wouldn't have shut it out, would you?"

Well, how far did he really want to push it? "Perhaps not."

"Oh, I'm sure you wouldn't have. But to get to the point of my call. I really need to discuss with you what's going on with Miss Speddon's things. You couldn't possibly stop here after work, could you? I'm still in her house till it's sold. There's only the caretaker and me, but I could give you a drink."

"I'd love to see that house," he exclaimed, with genuine enthusiasm. "And have a look at her treasures."

"You mean what's left of them. I'm afraid you'll be sadly disillusioned. About six, then?"

When she rang off, he resumed his contemplation of the snake, half-ashamed at his own satisfaction at being exonerated for the fate of the cat. But there was no denying that she had hurt him badly in that matter — and why? Because he blamed himself for what he had done? Of course not. He wouldn't have given a damn if that cat had starved. The world was full of cats. And yet he had hated appearing a brute to this girl. Why? Because he respected her judgment of men? Hardly. Had she not once admired Addams? Might she not still? Because he had fallen in love with her? That was hardly his style. Or was it simply that he was afraid, if he started caring about the things she cared about, that he would turn into the kind of nut that refused to swat a mosquito?

But he wasn't concentrating on the snake. The man who had made it could have been forgiven the massacre of a thousand cats for his carving of one. Had not even the priests felt that? Surely the artisan had been exempted from the bloodletting and human sacrifice of the time. Would Leo X have burned Raphael for even the most egregious heresy, or Henry VIII put his bloody paws on Holbein?

"Well, if the curator won't come to the director, I guess the director must come to the curator."

And there was Addams grinning in the doorway. Oh, for the crimson altar, the obsidian knife!

"I see you have put away all traces of your uncrating," Mark continued.

"Oh, I am always very neat, very tidy," Carol retorted blandly. "What can I do for you, Herr Direktor?"

"You can talk to me about that serpent. You needn't tell me how you got it. I already know."

Mark seated himself now in the chair opposite Carol and placed on his desk, so that it faced the curator, a typed sheet under the engraved letterhead of the Mexican Consulate.

Carol disdained to more than glance at the document. "I bought it in Zürich. You can rest assured that the museum got unimpeachable title."

"But it was illegally exported."

"So? Do they claim it was stolen?"

"Not in so many words. They claim it was smuggled out of the country."

"The purchaser in good faith of a smuggled item has good title. The offended nation is left with its remedy at law against the smuggler."

Mark's look was quizzical. "And that doesn't give you any trouble? Buying hot stuff?"

"It depends on what you call hot. A great many artifacts turn up on the auction block that have been taken out of Turkey or

China or Mexico, or where have you, without due observance of all border formalities. Many come through because custom officers — or perhaps even higher authorities — have been bribed. Is it our duty to maintain clean government in the Third World? That's quite a job you have given yourself, Mr. Director."

"But don't you see, Carol, you're encouraging the illegal traffic in works of art?"

"How could works of art be better cared for than in the great museums? Didn't Lord Elgin see the Turkish militia taking pot shots at the friezes in the Parthenon?"

"What about the dealers who dynamite archeological sites as the quickest way to unearth stuff they can sell?"

Carol glared at that hated boyish face. He always found the dynamiting argument distressing. "What do you propose to do with my snake?"

"Send it back to Mexico."

Carol jumped up in dismay. "But we own it, Addams!"

"Then we'll own it in Mexico."

"You can't do that! It belongs to the museum. Who do you think you are, anyway, that you can dispose of the collection?"

"I'll submit it to the board, of course."

"We'll see what Claverack will say to that."

"We'll also see what Peter Hewlett will say. He has promised me his backing in all such questions of restitution."

Carol went to the window and stared out despairingly at the park. Of course Addams was right about the chairman. Claverack would never oppose Hewlett over a jade snake. Oh, yes, he might take up the cudgels if it were a question of giving up some modern canvas of a naked old man with his balls for a head and a head for his balls, but confronted with something beautiful, something perfect . . . what did any of them care?

"Well, I hope you'll be satisfied when my vision serpent turns up at the Met or the Natural History. *They* won't be so fussy."

"I think you'll find they will be. There's a new spirit abroad, Carol."

"And I despise it! Why worry about the degenerate heirs of great civilizations? What do they know or care about their glorious predecessors? And what do *you*, Mark Addams? What are you but a cheap huckster who ripped off the misguided old virgin who put her faith in you? You talk to me of ethics? *You?*"

Mark had turned very red; his fists were clenched. "I'd better get out of here before I smack your yellow face."

"Yeah. You'd better."

"And get that snake ready for shipment. Today! And I'll be making a study of every damn thing you've bought since you've been with the museum."

"Do that. Clear the galleries for the pink garbage cans and plastic urinals of Claverack's Modern America wing. That's what he made you director for, isn't it?"

Still trembling with indignation, minutes after Mark had stamped from the room, Carol was nonetheless able to reflect, with a hard dry little chuckle, that Addams would never dare to fire him now. The director was too "virtuous" to wish to be tainted with a motive of personal resentment.

Seated with Anita in the long living room at 36th Street before a tray with half a bottle of whiskey and two tumblers — no hors d'oeuvres, he noted regretfully — he contemplated the bare spaces left by the removed portraits on the peeling walls.

"You'd think your great patroness had been dead a hundred years."

"Well, isn't that always the way with houses? They manage to put up a brave front, to stick it out so long as their owner is living, and then they suddenly go to pieces."

"And have the pictures all been sold?"

"Well, not, happily, the ones that were in this room. Even Claverack wanted to keep the Copleys. When they've been cleaned they'll be hung in the front hall of the museum."

"That's a relief. I thought we were going to get *Boy Masturbating in Swimming Tank* by his newest protégé."

"No, that will be the showpiece of the Modern America gallery. To be built with Speddon money, of course. But with nothing of hers in it but her portrait by Larry Rivers. The one that shows her as a kind of cipher in a gallery of empty frames."

"Hardly very kind."

"It's a work of art, anyway. Which is more than one will be able to say about its companions. Miss Speddon was always amused by it. But, then, she could take a joke about herself."

"What about the Speddon period rooms?"

"Some will be kept, but completely redecorated. The three main ones will be replaced by post–World War Two confections."

"And their contents?"

She shrugged. "Deaccessioned, I presume."

"What about the other things in this house? And the warehouse?"

"Well, the dolls, as you know, are already gone. And more than half the primitives. He did, I admit, keep some of the best of these, but that was thanks to Mrs. Pinchet."

"Who is?"

"The niece. Who has something of an eye. The nephew, Tom, is a complete philistine. More than half the silver and porcelain has been sold."

"But how can Claverack do that? Does he have the legal right?"

"It's not deaccessioning, you see. He claims he's acting under his broad powers as executor. The museum was left the artifacts, but the will gives him the power to define them."

"But isn't the nephew an executor, too?"

"Yes, but he's putty in Claverack's hands. He's a spendthrift who's gone through most of his own money and thinks he owes it to Claverack that he got a sixth of his aunt's estate. A notion that his co-executor does nothing to contradict. What he does owe to Claverack is his executorship and the big commissions he'll get for doing nothing but keeping his mouth shut. And incidentally there's a special provision in the will that all the art is commissionable."

"How can he do that? Isn't it a specific legacy?"

"Not if the testatrix provides otherwise. I suppose he convinced her that sorting out all those artifacts was work for which her executors should receive extra compensation. Which I wouldn't mind if he was sorting them out for the museum."

"And the nephew just nods."

"And holds his hand out. The only job he has is purporting to represent his aunt's point of view if any question is raised by the trustees at the museum. That is why Claverack put him on the board."

"Anita, do you realize that you have just described a criminal conspiracy?"

"And one that seems to be foolproof."

"What about the niece? Any hope there?"

"Not that I can see. She's very quiet, very staid, very old New York. The kind that leaves everything to 'the men.' "

"And her husband?"

"Not much better. When they go to Newport in the spring the one not driving holds in his lap the framed Abe Lincoln letter congratulating Arleus Speddon for his work on the Sanitary Commission. It's the same when they come back in the fall. The holy document is never trusted to a servant or left in an empty house."

"I see. It seems we have no remedy at law. At least not one that we've found yet. But there's no telling what you may discover once the mud starts flying."

"You don't expect me to throw mud, do you? What would Miss Speddon say? Would anything be worth *that* to her?"

"I'm surprised that after working for three years with a great collector you could ask so naïve a question. But relax. I don't mean mud we've made up. I mean real genuine, mucky, oozy, slimy, honest-to-God mud. What you've just told me!"

"How would we use it?"

"You and I would make a little call on my friend Bill Stebbins, the editor of *Art in Town.* He always appreciates a story of wicked fiduciaries. This will not, incidentally, be the first that he will owe me. I think it should make the cover."

Anita, who struck him as even paler and thinner than usual, or, as he preferred to put it, more agreeably pre-Raphaelite, turned away, slowly shaking her head. "I wonder if I could really bring myself to do that."

"And why not?" Carol was startled to hear the sudden rise in pitch of his own tone. "Is it because you might get Young Lochinvar into trouble? Well, let me say at once that I profoundly hope we may! Do you think for a minute that Addams hasn't been in this thing from the word go? Is there any toilet he wouldn't reach his dirty paws into at the behest of his lord and master?"

"Oh, Carol, please!"

"Well, *is* there?"

"It's so nice, our being friends again. I can't bear to have you all angry and cruel the way you used to be."

"Cruel? Who is crueler: Lochinvar or me? Did I make goo-goo eyes at you to worm my way into the confidence of your dear old mistress, who was beginning to dote? Did I?"

"Of course not."

"I'll bet he even made love to you." As Anita turned back to him with eyes that beseeched him to stop, he suddenly recalled the chilling of relations between her and Addams that had followed Miss Speddon's death. "I'll bet he even asked you to marry him!" It all came to him now in a shattering blaze, and he almost shouted, "At least he promised Miss Speddon he'd marry you, didn't he?"

"Carol, don't!"

"Didn't he?"

"Something like that."

Getting up, he took her by the shoulders and shook her. "Anita Vogel, it's your bounden duty, before whatever God may be, to tell the truth, and not to tell it slant, either, as the great Emily wrongfully suggested, but to tell it so that all the world shall know!"

She broke away from his grasp. "Oh, Carol, must I?"

"If you don't, it's because you love the son of a bitch! You'll be like one of those brutalized Nazi victims kneeling down to kiss her guard's toe!"

She sighed deeply as she had to give in. "All right, Carol. I'll go with you to your friend."

He kept his eye severely on her as he finished his drink in silence. "I'll set up an appointment with Stebbins and call you tomorrow."

10

SIDNEY CLAVERACK, now only two years short of his sixtieth birthday, had conceded finally to himself that his success in life — at least by his own standards — was going to be measured, if at all, by what he would achieve as chairman of his museum. He had had greater goals in the past, to be sure: a high court appointment, the Senate, even a fortune; but these had not and now would not be realized. His managing partnership in a middle-sized law firm was all very well, but certainly no great shakes in the league to which he had aspired, and some people were always going to say he owed it to his father, as they had in the past no doubt said that his father had owed it to his. The Claveracks and their firm, specializing in the administration of the estates of prosperous New York burghers, went back to the eighteen forties, and Sidney had tended to think of his male forebears as gentle altar boys tending the constantly lit and relit candles of the new rich. But if he were ever to stand out from that dim, respectable line, there was only one way still open: to have revitalized, nay, to have remade — to have in fact created

— a great cultural institution. That might not earn one the plaudits of the mob — never, it is true, to be despised — but it would surely merit the approval of a minority so esteemed for its discrimination as to become in due time the opinion of the many.

His father had always taught him: "A proper ambition is to *do* something, not just to *be* somebody." But Sidney even as a boy had never for a minute believed that anyone, including his didactic parent, had given more than lip service to such a dictum. No, the essence — the quintessence, indeed — of ambition was to be, or rather be always becoming, "somebody," and Sidney had never known real happiness except at those times when he could rest the burden of his thoughts and emotions on the step of a stairway that he knew he could continue to ascend any moment he chose. Always, when deprived of that blessed sense of being about to rise further, of still being, whatever the nature or duration of the pause, "on his way," he would become tense, depressed and ultimately, if the situation did not change, despairing.

Only once had he sought an explanation for this need of a constantly salted immediate future, and that was after his loss of the Senate race, when some nasty questions had been raised in the press as to the nature of his fund-raising. He had been sufficiently confounded to suspect that his mental processes were not so normal as he had supposed, and he had consulted a popular psychiatrist, author of the best-selling *Your Ego and My Id,* not for deep analysis, or even for free association lying on a couch — for he had no desire to have even a doctor poking into his subconscious — but simply to discuss openly the observable, ascertainable facts of his background and upbringing.

Dr. Klinger, a Freudian, made much of Sidney's father's judgeship. When he learned that Surrogate Claverack had married late and been elevated to the bench early, he could not resist the conclusion that Sidney as a little boy (and an only child at that) must have formed the image of a terrifying parent robed in billowing black who, with a few stabbing scratches of a pen, could send even a son — or perhaps particularly a son — to the grim chair with the hanging straps. Sidney had pointed out that his father's court had been without criminal jurisdiction, and that, taken early into the confidence of his kindly progenitor, he had known the mundane nature of the latter's judicial duties from childhood. He had even explained to Klinger that for the scion of a Knickerbocker family like Judge Claverack to have achieved a seat on the bench in a Tammany-dominated town had required a personality prone to jokes and winning smiles rather than one disposed to frowns and Olympian pronouncements. But the good doctor had simply pounced on this. What was more formidable to a child than the beaming geniality of a big, strong man, or more alarming than to see that grizzled head lowered to address one or to watch those flashing eyes behind the glittering pince-nez and to hear that booming "How now, my little man"?

Klinger, being Jewish, also tended to find a deeply inhibiting force in what he called the "stiff, tight, Upper East Side Protestant social enclave" of the Claveracks, and when Sidney had again explained his father's many political affiliations and his mother's humbler origin (she had been the trained nurse of his paternal grandmother), he had revised his opinion only to add a certain "social confusion" to his patient's obvious insularity. And when Sidney had gone on to argue that his father, in the interests of a possible political career for his son, had taught him to avoid the anglicized speech of his contemporaries and to adopt at least a moderate version of the voice of the people, the adaptable medical man had promptly riposted that to send a boy off to a snobbish New England preparatory school with a Brooklyn accent had been almost to guarantee his future insecurity.

When Klinger persisted, despite his patient's objections, in seeking to turn to the inquiry of early manifestations of sexuality, including contacts with other boys at boarding school, Sidney discontinued the sessions, not because such episodes had been lacking in the monastic academy which he had attended for four long years, but because he had no desire to make a record of them. Who could tell, after all, in an age of ever widening congressional investigation, what files, hitherto deemed confidential, might not be torn from their cabinets and exhibited to a gleeful public?

And so he had no explanation of the drives in school, college and law school that had pushed him down such different avenues towards such varying goals. He had tried the standard one of athletics to the standard end of popularity, until recurrent attacks of asthma had deflected him to the pursuit of high grades. When at Yale he discovered that these added little to a man's social prestige, he turned his efforts to parties and good times, cultivating a languid social manner and a cynical wit, and when at Yale Law School he found that seriousness was now the style, he worked assiduously and successfully to attain an editorship of the *Law Journal.* But if he always did well, the top positions, to which he aspired so passionately, eluded him. He was an editor but not the chief editor, as at preparatory school he had been a prefect but not the senior prefect, and as at Yale he had been elected to Wolf's Head but not to Skull and Bones. And this continued throughout his life. He became a state but not a United States senator, as in his oil ventures he made a million but not ten. It was why the Museum of North America had begun to seem his last chance to make the big league.

Sometimes he thought it was because he never seemed to be able to let himself go "all out" in any one field. It was as if he had to be holding something back, to be persistently hedging his bets. This was certainly true of his personal relations. Although so long as she lived he was always at ease with his adoring, plain, sensible, simple old mother, and even with the benign, uncritical father whose high opinion of him, he perfectly realized, was as unchangeable as it was undeserved, he was never really close to any other humans of either sex. With men his relationships went little further than jokes and story-swapping, and with women he was apt to cultivate the appearance rather than the actuality of romance. He would take out only the most popular and sought-after girls, who enjoyed his wit and high spending and would often use him as a foil in their game of catching one of his even more eligible companions.

When he did marry it was to just the kind of girl he had pictured in the most secret corner of his mind, the very opposite of what he would have liked to boast about to other bachelors, plain but by no means ugly, of a disposition calm to the point of dullness, who was never going to try to take him apart and thereby incur the risk of not being able to put him together again. She seemed to accept him as he was and gave all the appearance of allowing him to do his own things and to think his own thoughts while she raised their two children with faultless care. Helena Ballard, the rather crushed product of dowdy but respectable parents, had, with the instinct of certain girls of solid but impecunious brownstone background, always been sure that an acceptable husband would one day present himself. That he should have some kind of inward or outward flaw to make him seek out such a one as Helena Ballard was taken quite for granted. The only thing that disgruntled Sidney, in the two and a half decades of his marriage to this woman of whose strength of character he became increasingly and at times uncomfortably aware, was that she never once showed the smallest curiosity as to what that flaw was.

He had first approached modern art, like so many men of affairs, as an investment. If fortunes could be made out of artists such as Motherwell, Pollock and de Kooning, who had been bargains only decades back, it was obvious that the process could be repeated. He never attempted to select for himself among unknown painters in the Village or in Chelsea, but he paid fees to dealers to keep an eye out for him, and little by little he began to buy. He would hang his purchases in his office, or in parts of the apartment where his wife did not object too vociferously, and he would listen silently with a shrug or half-smile as his friends made the usual banal jokes about them. He never tried to defend his art, nor did he even wish to. It made almost as little sense to him as it did to his guests.

Almost. And then, on a visit to an exhibition of amateur abstract painters at his bar association, he had what he afterwards deemed a species of near mystic revelation. He had hitherto doubted (without admitting his doubts to anyone) that there could be any valid criterion for judging an abstract. If it didn't have to look like anything, how could one say it was well or poorly executed? But what struck him that day was that the paintings in that hall, some of them by men he knew and respected, were the most wretched of daubs. They were dead, dead as Queen Anne, if mortality and English queens had any application to nonrepresentational art.

Which had to mean, did it not, that other abstracts could be living? At home he re-examined his purchases and decided that he was now in a position to choose among them. He found that he liked some color arrangements, some groupings, some figures, and disliked others. Without even asking himself why, he sent the ones that did not meet with his favor back to the dealers, and hung the rest more prominently about the apartment. Helena made rather a fuss, but only a slight one, really. Basically, she never looked at a picture of any kind.

And now he began to actually enjoy buying pictures. It was a solitary pleasure, as he did not have any friend close enough to share it with, but of what pleasure in his life had that not been true? He never bought a picture that was not recommended by a dealer he trusted, but he felt free now to reject many that were. As a collector he exercised only a veto power. He avoided discussions of modern art; he could not even pretend to understand them. He put his trust in his peculiar star, and that celestial body seemed to favor him. Less than a decade after the visit to the bar association gallery he was known in metropolitan artistic circles as a minor, eccentric but on the whole respected purchaser of contemporary art.

When he ultimately decided to unite his two central interests by promoting the development of modern art at the Museum of North America, he felt a thrill in the sensation that here, at long last, was the key that fitted the lock that would turn — oh, so easily and smoothly, and with such a divinely welcoming click! — to open the portal to the "first" position which had so far eluded him. And indeed, with the Speddon will he seemed not only to have passed through those gates but to be roaming at will in his own Garden of Eden!

He even found himself for the first time giving tongue to a principle. It was at a press conference after the public announcement of the expansion plan of the museum, when he was asked this question: "Isn't your new museum, Mr. Claverack, going to be somewhat out of proportion? It will be more than half contemporary. How do you reconcile that with your basic function of illustrating the history of North America?"

"Isn't it a question of whether you look at history horizontally or vertically? Suppose you are telling the story of a family. There's a grandfather, say, a son and eight grandchildren. Do those eight grandchildren occupy one third or eight tenths of your story?"

"You mean if the thirteen colonies had a population of four million at the time of the Revolution, they'd only get that fraction of space — let's see. What's four million over our population today?"

"That's it! There may be more people living at the present time than have died in recorded history. Or at least we're getting to that point."

"But aren't you saying, sir, that the past is too thinly populated to be worth bothering about? Aren't you throwing history out the window? Is there no question of quality? Surely the city of Florence produced more great art in one generation than the whole continent of South America has since the days of the Incas. How did Tennyson put it? 'Better fifty years of Europe than a cycle of Cathay'?"

"Provided you take the last fifty years."

The publicity that followed this statement was more than any he had gotten since his Senate campaign. Nobody could entirely discount Sidney Claverack now. Even Helena.

Or perhaps only Helena. She had a way, for all her indifference to her spouse's major interests, of poking an occasionally probing finger into sensitive areas. How she divined the whereabouts of these he couldn't tell; it had to be a kind of instinct. This happened on a morning at breakfast in the exciting week when he received the blueprints for his museum master plan. She had put down her coffee cup and gazed across the table at him with placid, patient eyes until, unable to feign a further absorption in his paper, he had looked up. Her oblong face and oval chin, so oddly squared by her straight black hair and bangs, were immobile to the point of menace.

"Your cousin Lucy Pinchet told me a funny thing yesterday."

"Oh? Where did you see Lucy?"

"At the Colony Club. I was waiting for Molly Spears at lunch time when Lucy came over. She said to warn you there was an article coming out in the next issue of *Art in Town*. Something about Cousin Daisy's estate and undue influence and I don't know what else."

He had a sudden searing vision of Miss Vogel, nude, skinny, bound to a tree and pierced with arrows. An ugly, anguished, female Sebastian. He drew another arrow from his quiver.

"I guess I should have listened to Addams."

"What has he got to do with it?"

"He said we shouldn't have fired the Vogel woman. Of course this is all her spite."

"Then it's not true? You're not really selling all Cousin Daisy's things?"

He looked at her more sharply now. Had she actually read that article?

"Well, of course, we've had to do a good deal of weeding out. Cousin Daisy had a very eclectic collection and a lot of it not of the first rank. Which was why she gave me such wide discretion."

"Really? It doesn't sound like her at all. I thought she thought everything she bought was an absolute treasure. Right down to the last buttonhook and thimble."

"Why are you taking such a great interest in Cousin Daisy all of a sudden? It was all I could do to get you to call on her while she was alive."

"Well, I never could stand her old maid sentimentality and her drooling over beautiful things. That kind of frustrated lesbianism I had quite enough of as a girl, thank you very much, when Mother shipped me off to stay with the maiden aunts in Northeast Harbor. But family is family, after all, and if we're going to be smeared all over the public prints . . ."

"One article in a low-circulation art magazine is hardly being smeared in the public prints."

"Well, so long as you say so. But I'd hate to have people insinuating we hadn't done right by Cousin Daisy."

Sidney knew that he was now on notice, if it came to a row, which side his wife would be on. For Helena was a tribal creature. She was a loyal enough spouse, but her primary duty would always be to the chief medicine man. So long as Sidney remained strictly within the rules of the village, she would obey him. But the moment he strayed, she would, with an appalling impassivity, hand him over to voodoo for whatever emasculation was prescribed.

In his dressing room, getting ready for the office, he tried to reduce the matter to its correct proportions. After all, the will had been admitted to probate, the estate half-administered and court approval obtained for the major sales and distributions. What could the Vogel bitch do but whimper? A little public whimpering would soon pass. And in the meantime he had his plan, his master plan! The outline in white lines on blue paper of what would soon be soaring arches and marble walls! Nothing must be allowed to destroy his pleasure in the realization of his bold decision to reorient the entire museum into a chronological series of galleries culminating in the great Modern America wing. What a glory it was going to be, with its political, religious and scientific exhibits, its documents and dioramas and splendid artifacts, climaxing in the giant comic strip cartoon dramatizing the coincidence in time of the moon landing and the tragedy of Chappaquiddick!

On his way to the subway, which he always took to Grand Central, he bought a copy of *Art in Town.* He saw at once that the article was a good deal worse than he had feared; the ride was not nearly long enough to finish it. At his office he closed his door and told his secretary he would take no calls.

Its title was "The Conning of Evelyn Speddon." The first page of the piece faced a full page of photographs: of Miss Speddon, of the façade of the museum, of Mark Addams and of Sidney himself. The text told of Mark's calls on the old lady during her last illness and prior to the execution of a new will, only weeks before her demise. It strongly implied that Addams had given the testatrix the impression that he was romantically interested in her ward. It ended with a partial list of the sales made by the executors and the museum, and a prediction of extensive deaccessioning in the future.

Sidney brooded for a silent hour. Even when his mind was seething, it could still work closely on a problem. What, after all, was this but the work of the same old imp, grinning in the path before him, that had leaked the story of the cribbed term paper at Yale which had cost him his bid to Skull and Bones, and tipped off the *New York Times* to the illegal campaign contribution? So long as one knew in time, damage could often be contained. He had been able to put about his own version of the term paper story so as to salvage a bid from another senior society, and to handle the campaign trouble in a way to avoid all danger of indictment. Half-truths, quarter-truths lost much of their menace once one was apprised of their circulation. As here now. Oh, yes, the article might even turn out to be a blessing in disguise, a warning that he had been going a bit too far in the Speddon matter, a small malignant tumor that was still operable, that could very likely be excised, completely encapsulated in untainted flesh. He picked up the telephone.

"Call Mrs. Pinchet," he told his secretary, "and ask her if she'd be so kind as to receive me in half an hour. She'll know what it's about."

Lucy Pinchet's house, on East 80th Street, small, neat and Georgian, was as cool and exquisite as its owner's manners. There were Victorian things in it — perhaps even ugly ones — Belter chairs and Bouguereaus — but the perfect condition of every piece produced a kind of harmony. Lucy, pale, plump and still pretty, received him with a little smile that could have meant almost anything. But it was no doubt significant that no kind of refreshment was offered.

"I've come about the article."

"Of course."

"Do you think I should sue? Or simply take an attitude of high disdain?"

"If you were to sue, what would you sue for?"

"Why, damages for libel, of course."

"But isn't libel the remedy for misrepresentation?"

"Certainly."

"Then what facts does the article distort?"

Sidney paused to redeploy his forces. He even found a moment in which to wonder what he had done to unite the sex against him. Vogel, his wife and now Lucy. What was it in Sidney Claverack that turned them into termagants?

"Why, simply every fact there is! The article is a tissue of lies from start to finish. It is manifestly the product of revenge. Miss Vogel was discharged by the museum for insolence and insubordination."

"For *alleged* insolence and insubordination."

"Lucy, can you really have had the time to come to serious conclusions about that piece? It only just came out."

"But I received it in galleys two weeks ago. The editor submitted it to Miss Vogel, and she brought it to me. I have had every opportunity to study it. And to discuss it with some of Aunt Daisy's old friends." She paused to smile with a deadly sweetness. Obviously she was having the time of her life. "*And* with my lawyers. My new lawyers. Selders and Stein. For I hardly thought it would be possible to retain your firm when you will be a defendant. One of the defendants, I should say. My brother, Tom, will be another, though he seeks to be co-plaintiff. And of course I shall 'join,' as I believe the legal term is, the Museum of North America and its enterprising but, I'm afraid, unscrupulous young director."

Sidney began to feel reassurance in the prickle of combat. He summoned up a picture of a squadron of bullet-headed soldiers in brown uniform dragging a stripped Lucy down to a cold dripping cellar to machine-gun her bloated body against a wall.

There was no hint of this, however, in what he smoothly said: "If you think you can upset Cousin Daisy's will, let me remind you that it has been duly admitted to probate pursuant to your own duly executed waiver and consent."

"I am of course aware, Sidney, that with a firm as able as yours, every form has been scrupulously followed. The bone that I am picking with you is with your morals, not your mind. You will shortly be served with a summons and complaint instructing you that I intend to prove a conspiracy between you and Tom and your director to take advantage of Aunt Daisy's enfeebled mind. I shall allege that you substituted a will that she never understood for the one that set forth her true intentions. As for my waiver and consent, of course they were obtained by fraud."

Sidney was still able to smile and shake his head. "You will find the game on which you have embarked an expensive one. However, I suppose I shouldn't begrudge a good fee to a fellow member of the bar. I've always had the greatest respect for Harold Stein."

In the taxi crossing the park to the museum, Sidney carefully thought out his defense plan. When the driver spoke of the heat of the early spring, he shut him up. He had already been back to his office, and after a conference with Miss Norton he was beginning to make out the possibility of placing the onus of the Speddon "conspiracy" squarely on the shoulders of the director. That had not indeed been Norton's idea. But wasn't it with Addams that the ultimate responsibility *should* lie? Had Addams not recently been hinting that the chairman was impinging on the director's territory? Well, that young man would find one territory that he could have entirely to himself!

Which was only right, too. Sidney glanced at a flock of pigeons swooping down to an old woman scattering crumbs. Were they poisoned crumbs? One read of such witches. Surely Lucy Pinchet would be capable of it. The trustees were supposed to be aloof, dignified, unchanging in temper. They should be kept clear of coprophagous bugs like Lucy, scrounging for extra legacies in the dung of the Surrogate's Court. That was surely the director's business.

And if Lucy were defeated, would he not have a permanent hold on Addams from the way it had been done? Would Addams not have to perjure himself? Oh, yes, he *was* beginning to see his way. And his duty as well! One had to be tough in all businesses, and cultural institutions were no exception.

He did not go to Mark's office at the museum. He went to the smaller one reserved for the chairman and rarely occupied, and sent word to Mark to join him there. It was a time to observe every hierarchical distinction.

Mark came in, a copy of *Art in Town* in hand, and took a seat opposite the chairman without even a greeting, his expression accepting grimly the gravity of the conference about to be held. Sidney began.

"I have just come from Lucy Pinchet. She is going to sue. Undue influence, fraud, the works."

"I supposed that was in the cards."

"I thought I'd put Chessie Norton on the case. She's a tough litigator, and this will be her great chance."

A pause. "Of course, you know of our relationship."

"I thought that was over. Anyway, she knows all about you and Miss Vogel."

"What is there to know?"

"Isn't that for the jury, my friend?"

Sidney surveyed with some satisfaction the troubled countenance before him. What *had* happened between Mark and the Vogel woman? Had he really slept with the scrawny creature? Probably. Didn't these young men screw everything that moved?

"A couple of kisses, that was all."

"Well, it had better be a case of kissing and *not* telling."

"May I ask you what you mean by that?"

"You may. In fact, I think it an excellent idea for you and me to cultivate the habit of frankness with each other. We may find it useful in the months ahead. I presume that any osculations between you and Miss Vogel did not occur before a grossly gaping public. That they happened in the privacy of your apartment or hers?"

Mark was very red now, but whether from anger or shame was not clear. "Certainly not in public. But as I've never been in Miss Vogel's apartment, nor she in mine, I suppose whatever happened took place in a taxi."

"So unless the driver is identifiable, it will be her word against yours?"

"Surely Mrs. Pinchet's counsel won't go into trivia like that?"

"It's precisely what they *will* do, unless they want Lucy to charge them with malpractice. They'll try to establish a sinister plot to undermine an ancient, addled testatrix. You must take the position before the judge and jury that nothing occurred between Galahad Addams and Virgin Vogel that would not have taken place before a synod of bishops!"

"Won't that make me seem an awful ass?"

"But an innocent ass, my boy. An innocent ass."

Mark got up impatiently and went to the window. "At the risk of saying 'I told you so,' may I point out that I begged you not to fire Miss Vogel?"

"No, sir, you may not. Because when I dispensed with her services, I had no idea that our virtuous director had been snatching kisses from her pretty lips."

"Hadn't you virtually suggested it?"

"Never!"

"Hadn't you practically told me to get Miss Speddon to change her will any way I could? Hadn't you even promised me the directorship if I succeeded?"

Sidney, contemplating the mottled features of this angry young man, was almost enjoying himself.

"You must know, Mark, that I have a very emphatic, at times even an exaggerated, way of putting things. No doubt, in speaking to you about using your arts of persuasion on the late Miss Speddon, I may have seemed to suggest that you climb into the old girl's bed, let alone her companion's. But that is what my friends call Sidney's hyperbole. The means were left entirely to your discretion. It certainly never crossed my mind that they would not be altogether proper and ethical."

Mark's stare showed that he saw he was trapped. "Would it

be 'proper and ethical' for me to perjure myself by denying something I'd done?"

"Perjury? It's a strong word. Look at it this way. What, in theory at least, will a court of law be trying to establish? The truth, will it not? Now you and I both know that the truth is that Miss Speddon was of sound mind when she executed that will. Don't you agree?"

"Yes, but —"

"Yes but nothing. She may have had some old maid's bee in her bonnet about a romance between you and her protégée, but when you get right down to it, she knew who her heirs were, what the terms of her will were, and how it would operate. Is that not certainly so?"

Mark played with the shade cord. "Yes, I guess that is so."

"Very well. Then it is up to us to help the court establish that truth. If you admit that in the course of your discussions with Miss Speddon you made cynical love to her confidante, you are going to cast the whole business in a very ugly light. The jury will see you as a cool and calculating villain and may well be persuaded that you bamboozled the old girl into doing something she really didn't want to do."

"So I must tell a lie to establish a truth?" Mark resumed his seat before the desk. "Frankly, Sidney, your attitude strikes me as unacceptably cynical. I know you care for the museum as much as I do, and I know how much I owe you. But a man's got to make his own moral decisions. The fact that I may have once made some wobbly ones doesn't mean they all have to be wobbly. And I wonder whether the time hasn't come for me to be truthful at any cost."

"At any cost?" Sidney moistened his lips as he touched with one finger the shiny surface of the ace of trumps in his imagined hand. "Any cost to whom? To yourself or the museum?"

"Well, would it really be such a great cost to the museum to make a compromise with Miss Speddon's relatives about the disposition of her things? I think you know, sir, that I have had doubts about your handling of that situation."

Sidney, taking in the new air of resolution in those now unblinking eyes, reflected that perhaps this lawsuit had come in the very nick of time. The real enemy might not be Vogel or even Lucy, after all! "If we lose this case, my boy, there won't be any Speddon things to worry about. Or Speddon money, either. Except what the old girl gave us in her lifetime, and even that may be in question."

"I don't follow you."

"It's very simple. Mrs. Pinchet is trying to knock out her aunt's will. If she succeeds, Miss Speddon will have died intestate, which means that everything she owned will be divided between her niece and nephew. Which is why, incidentally, Tom Speddon, who has hitherto been my greatest ally, can now be counted on for the Judas kiss. Indeed, the case promises to be full of kisses."

"But why is that? If a will goes down, isn't the previous will substituted? Don't you have dozens of earlier Speddon wills in your vault?"

Sidney made a circle with his thumb and forefinger. "Not one. Miss Speddon had a fetish about destroying the old will each time she executed a new one. She had a horror of legatees about whom she'd changed her mind — giving Cousin Harriet the lavalière she'd once given Cousin Tillie — finding out about it."

"So even if you settle the case, you've got to save the will?"

"The very existence of the museum may depend on it. If that will goes down, Mark Addams, it will be you and you alone who will have struck the fatal blow at our beloved institution!"

"Aren't you going rather far there, Mr. Claverack?"

"Not an inch too far, Mr. Addams."

"You would share none of the responsibility?"

"None. Because if undue influence is proved, it will be *your* undue influence, not mine. *You* were the man who talked her into signing that new will. You were the person who chose the means to do it. Had you not intervened, her will of a year earlier would have been probated, and the museum would have received the collection plus millions of dollars. Under onerous conditions, it is true, but that would be a hell of a lot better than zilch."

The flicker now in those gray-green eyes was something like agony. "But do you deny altogether that it was your idea?"

"Why should I deny anything? I simply indicated to you that it would be a very agreeable thing if the museum were to receive its bequest unconditionally. What chairman of a board of trustees would have felt otherwise? It was *you* who undertook the project of implementing what had been a mere wish on my part. And in choosing your means you had to take the responsibility for their success or failure. I charge you, Mark Addams, with the moral duty of doing everything in your power to sustain that will!"

Mark sat still, brooding, and made no answer. Sidney rose and took his hat from the pole. "I shall tell Miss Norton to call you as soon as the *lis pendens* has been filed."

11

MARK, sitting in Chessie's bare, clean cell of an office, with its gleaming fresh gray paint and its sole ornament, a print of bland-faced, thinly smiling Lord Mansfield, proud in wig and robe, reflected ruefully that his one-time lover had the advantage of him. Her desk was clear of all papers but the court documents of *Pinchet v. Claverack et al.*, neatly piled on the blotter before her and surely too well previously studied to be really needed. Over them her long Modigliani face and straight red hair presented an aspect as coolly judicial as the engraving above.

"Have you had any difficulty in being represented by me?"

"Not really. I know you're capable of separating yourself from any emotional involvement in the past. If there *was* any."

"What the hell do you mean by that?"

"Well, forgive me, Chessie, but you seem so — so legal, if that's the word, that I can hardly believe that some things ever happened."

He suddenly realized that he meant it. Had he actually been in bed with this woman? It was as if he were a randy kid brought up on charges of playing dirty games in the barn before a stern teacher who in some mad fashion had also been the detective disguised as the lusty girl who had entrapped him.

"Oh, they happened all right." The teacher was even smiling now. "And I don't regret them. I hope you don't?"

"Oh, no."

"Then we can work together? With no reservations?"

"None. Except some people at the museum think it odd that Claverack should use his own firm for the defense."

"It's unusual. But perfectly proper. And if the right detachment exists between Claverack and myself, there's nothing against it."

"You don't even much like the guy, as I recall."

"That is true. But I think I understand him, which is more important. And I have no doubt that you and he should win this case."

He noted the flicker of a spark in her eye. "Which will be to your professional advantage?"

"It should make me a partner in this shop. Isn't that all to the good? Shouldn't your lawyer be strongly motivated?"

He considered it. "But do you really want to be a partner of Claverack's?"

"Does that matter? Once I'm a member of this firm I can go anywhere I want."

"Then let me tell you this, counsellor. I intend to deny absolutely that I ever made any sort of a pass at Anita Vogel."

"Of course."

The stare with which she met his was the signal that he was not to go on. A reputable lawyer could have nothing to do with perjury.

"Then that is understood. And knowing what Claverack knows about me — or thinks he knows about me — can't you imagine what my future at the museum is going to be? With him always able to mutter: 'Remember the Speddon case, my boy. We got you out of that one with a fairly clean nose, but if you give me any trouble . . .' "

"But you know as much about him as he does about you."

"Ah, but he doesn't care!"

Chessie frowned. She was not liking the turn of the conversation. "I wish you wouldn't fret about the future. These things will probably take care of themselves. A worried witness is going to be a bad one."

"I won't be a worried witness, Chessie."

"Can I count on that?"

"Oh, surely."

"Why so surely?"

"Because I want you to win and be a partner."

"But that's charming of you, Mark!" The quick smile made her look almost girlish. "I appreciate it very much." She looked down for some moments at the papers on her desk, but he could see she was not thinking of them. She seemed to be concentrating on something quite different. When she looked up, her lips were pursed in doubt. Then she nodded in sudden decision. "All right, I'll tell you something. Something that may give you a bit of a hold on the great Sidney."

"Is there a corpse he's hidden?"

"Not hidden; that's the point. Check the appraisals of all of the gifts that clients of his have made to the museum."

He stared. "Do we have them?"

"Yes. He always sent copies to the museum files."

"And what will I find?"

"Oh, that's your affair. I think I've done quite enough already. More than enough, as a matter of fact. Now let's get to work on your testimony for the examination before trial. For that's all we have these days, you know. The best lawyers never get to trial."

Mark found himself, in the days before the hearing, in a strange, hollow state of mind. It was as if his life had become a kind of villa by the sea, fine and handsome but vacated and boarded up for the winter, in which he had been left behind by "others" to roam in solitude its unheated halls and corridors. Everything had been cleaned and put in order for the cold season, the rare books in old gold bindings neatly arow on their shelves, the Venetian lacquered chairs with their backs to the wall, but the objects seemed to be waiting for him to leave so that they could take up some strange life of their own. Yet he couldn't leave. He could only pace the floors and stare out the windows at a bleak garden that didn't need him, didn't want him. Until a spring that might never come.

He wondered whether he had been too greedy about his life. He had chosen to enter the monastery of museum routine, but he seemed to have brought the world in with him, unless he had found it already there. He had had the temerity to worship success in the very temple of art, and Lucifer, in the fancy dress of Claverack, was laughing at him. Oh, screeching with laughter! He had everything he had asked for and didn't need to go to hell — he was already there! For what was hell but nothingness, deadness, the empty villa on the seashore? What else, in the name of all that was holy, if anything was, should he have expected?

The hollow days ended in the brown-paneled courtroom only faintly illuminated by the summer sunlight that peered in from high windows. Mark was conscious of nothing but the round features of the massive Harold Stein, whose shifting eyes seemed to bar forever the possibility of sympathy between men of Stein's rectitude and the witness's meanness. Mark knew that Chessie, sitting below him, was planning no objections. Her scheme, as she had told him, was to let the "great litigator" hang himself with his own oratory. Her client had been exhaustively coached. It was up to him now.

"On your visits to the late Miss Speddon, you had frequent occasion, did you not, to talk to Miss Vogel?"

"Certainly."

"I believe you were sometimes alone with her?"

"I was."

"And that you even took her out for dinner?"

"On one occasion."

"On what is called a date?"

"What *is* called a date, Mr. Stein?"

"We'll pass that. What did you and Miss Vogel usually talk about?"

"Oh, general things. Miss Speddon in particular, I guess."

"Not Miss Speddon's will?"

"No."

"Why not? That was the reason, was it not, for your visits to the decedent? To discuss the terms of a new will?"

"It was."

"Would it not have been natural for you to enlist Miss Vogel's sympathy in seeking a grant of wider discretion to the decedent's executors?"

"I had reason to believe that Miss Vogel was opposed to such a grant."

"I see. Then your relations with her were purely social?"

"We were associates at the museum."

"Was it to discuss museum matters, then, that you took her out to dinner?"

"Not particularly."

"Why then, if it was not to discuss either the museum or Miss Speddon's will, or, seemingly, for a 'date,' did you make such a point of cultivating Miss Vogel?"

Mark decided it was now time for that prepared show of indignation. "Because we were friends, Mr. Stein! Because Miss Vogel had a weary time looking after a sick old lady, and I wanted to supply her with some diversion and relaxation."

But Stein, too, was ready for the change of tone. "And was it to relax Miss Vogel that you kissed her?"

"I never kissed her."

"You didn't kiss her in the taxicab, coming home from the restaurant?"

"Certainly not."

"And you never kissed her in your office at the museum?"

"Never."

Mark was careful to make his tone plain, matter-of-fact, as if, anticipating this line of questioning, he was only doing his simple if tiresome duty of setting the record straight for a court that could not be expected to know how infamous the plaintiff's allegations were. Chessie had suggested that he taint his tone with a faint repulsion at the mere idea of physical intimacy with the plaintiff's witness, but he would not do that. He did not look at Anita, but he had seen her when he came into the chamber, sitting on a bench with Mrs. Pinchet, very stiff and still, her face a long blob of white with two deep black circles.

"What would you say, Mr. Addams, if I were to tell you that a stenographer in your office had witnessed one such kiss and that we were on the trail of a taxi driver who had seen another?"

"I'd say you were bluffing, Mr. Stein."

When he left the stand a few minutes later and took his seat beside Chessie, he could tell, by the very rigidity of her posture, that she was pleased by his performance.

Her turn came that afternoon when Anita was on the stand. Chessie seemed to tower over the hunched, nervous witness, her arms folded, a faintly sneering smile lurking about her lips.

"Miss Vogel, you have professed a great concern for the fate of the Speddon collection. Would you say that has been your principal interest in the past three years?"

"I think so."

"Could you please speak a little louder?"

"Yes, it has."

"And of course you have felt that inadequate care and attention have been given this collection by the Museum of North

America. But have you ever had occasion to consider what would happen to it if Miss Speddon's will were overturned?"

"Objection, Your Honor. Miss Vogel's speculations about the effect of intestacy on the decedent's possessions can hardly be relevant."

"I am attempting to impeach the witness's earlier testimony. I contend it would have been different had she had knowledge of certain facts."

Counsel were now summoned to the dais, where a whispered conference took place. Chessie evidently won her point, for when she returned to the witness stand she repeated her last question.

"I'm not a lawyer, Miss Norton. The estate would go to Mrs. Pinchet, would it not?"

"It would go to the heirs at law. Of whom Mrs. Pinchet is only one. Is that better, do you think, than having it go to a museum of which Miss Speddon was a devoted trustee and supporter most of her life?"

"Mrs. Pinchet has assured me that she would turn some of the collection over to the Colonial Museum."

"Assured you? And only some of it? And only some of her share? Is that better than having *all* of it go to the institution that her aunt surely favored in her lifetime? Is that what you intended to accomplish, Miss Vogel?"

This was followed by another stormy whispering session at the dais. Mark noted the deepening air of bewilderment on Anita's drawn countenance. Her eyes were fastened on Chessie's back and gesticulating arms. She seemed hypnotized. And he realized suddenly that Chessie had based all her tactics on the use of one terrible weapon: her assurance that Anita would tell the truth and that he wouldn't! She returned now to the witness.

"Tell me this, Miss Vogel. Did Mrs. Pinchet promise you that she would use her influence as a donor to the Colonial Museum to get you a job there looking after the Speddon things?"

"I think she did say something to that effect."

Mark almost jumped from his seat. How in God's name had Chessie known that? Or was it a wild gamble?

"I believe you were discharged from the Museum of North America?"

"I was. But —"

"Just answer the question, please. So, Miss Vogel, in return for a job supervising a mere handful of your patroness's artifacts you were willing to manufacture testimony that would destroy her entire testamentary plan. Quite a nice little revenge, isn't it, on the museum that fired you?"

This time, in answer to Stein's outraged objections, the judge reproved Chessie. But there was no repentance in her demeanor as she continued.

"Miss Vogel, you have read the deposition of Mrs. Kay?"

"I have."

"You will have noted, then, that she is of the firm opinion that the decedent was of sound mind to the very end. Is Mrs. Kay also, in your opinion, senile?"

"Oh, no. Not at all."

Chessie glanced significantly at the jury before continuing with a new attack.

"You have testified that Mr. Addams made love to you in an effort to worm his way into Miss Speddon's confidence. Had any other man so presumed on your affections during the time that you lived at Thirty-sixth Street?"

"At Miss Speddon's? Certainly not."

"That sounds emphatic. How long did you live there?"

"Three years."

"A good long time. So it was unusual for a male visitor to the house to pay you that kind of attention?"

"Oh, yes. Most of Miss Speddon's visitors were ladies."

"And very ladylike, I'm sure. It was an orderly household, was it not?"

"Very orderly."

"And not seeing men there, being isolated in the company of your own sex, would you say that you might have lost touch, to some extent anyway, with the usual behavior of attractive young males in society?"

"I don't think so. I wasn't always at Miss Speddon's."

"But didn't you usually go straight to work from there and straight home from work?"

"Yes."

"Did you ever have a date in all that time?"

"I don't suppose I did."

"Then might it not have been possible for you to mistake the normal gallantries of a young man in society for something more serious?"

"I don't think so."

"You don't? I suggest that your experience in romantic matters has been limited, Miss Vogel. Did you not once, before you came to Miss Speddon's, break your engagement to a man because he was unkind to a cat?"

"I wasn't engaged to him!"

"Excuse me. Did you decide not to become engaged to him because he was unkind to a cat?"

"He left it out in the street to starve!"

"Wasn't that because he had no place to keep it?"

"As if that was an excuse!"

"That will be all. Thank you, Miss Vogel."

Mark cursed himself for having told Chessie the silly story. He even hoped the jury might contain a cat lover who would take the episode as something other than a token of Anita's inexperience with men. But what a tigress Chessie was! To remember such details, to store them away in the law library of her mind for possible use in a court to stun some helpless mouse of a witness! When Anita passed in front of his bench, he could see that she was weeping. The judge recessed for the day, and Mark slipped out of the room without speaking to anyone.

But that night Chessie called him at his apartment, victory ringing in her voice.

"Oh, Mark, I've the most wonderful news! It seems Anita Vogel went bananas in Harold Stein's office and they had to cart her off to a sanitarium. I'm sorry if I was rough with her at the deposition, but all's fair in love and litigation."

"My God, poor Anita! Is she really in a bad way?"

"Oh, it's just a fit of nerves. They say she'll be fine in a day or so."

"Really? You *were* rough on her, Chessie."

"Well, she started it all. She was the one who got Pinchet to sue. And you know what they say about ill winds. This one may blow us right into port."

"You mean win the case?"

"I've already called Stein. I told him how concerned we were about Miss Vogel and that if the strain was too much for her and they wanted an honorable out, how about a settlement? How about their withdrawing their suit in return for the museum's pledge to name the new wing the Evelyn Speddon Gallery of Modern America?"

"You think they'll buy that?"

"Why not? Stein must know his case is shot. This gives his client the chance to claim a moral victory and issue a press release saying that all she really wanted was a proper recognition of what her aunt had done for the museum."

"And how will Claverack take it?"

"Well, he didn't like it. I'll tell you that. I'm sure he was planning to get his own name on that wing. But he saw that it fitted the bill. He had to go along."

"But Anita! What we've put her through."

"What she's put *you* through! From where I sit you two are even-steven."

He sighed. "Well, I guess there's one thing we can all agree on. That you, my dear, are a great lawyer."

"Oh, that tone! I guess I know what you think of lawyers, great or otherwise. How about coming over for a victory drink?"

He looked critically at the receiver and then shrugged. "Why not?"

She greeted him at the door, as in the old days, in pajamas under a black Chinese robe embroidered with gold flowers. In one hand she was holding a glass of champagne, which she pressed into his.

"To victory!"

"Any more word about Anita?"

She made a face. "I knew you'd ask, so I called the hospital. She's going to be fine. Just a slight collapse. She probably did it on purpose. Witnesses like that often do."

He stood by the fireplace and pensively drank the champagne while she watched him from the divan. On the round table between them was a plate of caviar. Chessie was obviously planning more than a celebration. Well, again, why not? Didn't she deserve it? Maybe poor Anita was only the egg that had to be broken for the making of Chessie's fluffy omelette. And if Anita really was going to be all right . . .

"You *were* hard on her."

"I was only doing my job. She shouldn't start things she can't finish. Don't be soppy about her, Mark. She did her best to do *you* in."

"I guess she had some reason."

"Well, shut up on that score. I don't want to hear any more about that."

"Oh, you lawyers! You do keep your fingers clean. Can I have some more champagne?"

"Take the whole bottle! And there's another on the ice. Unless you prefer whiskey. Oh, Mark, just think: the museum's safe, and you're safe, and I shall have my just reward, and everything's for the best in the best of all possible worlds!"

"Can this be the stern, realistic Miss Norton talking?"

"Oh, Miss Norton has her human moments. Just because she doesn't crumple up and burst into tears under cross-examination doesn't mean she has no feelings. But damn it all, let's not waste this wonderful evening talking about a drip like Vogel. Can't you and I get together again? I've missed you frightfully. There, it's out, and I'm glad of it. There hasn't been anyone since you, either. What really broke us up? What but my lousy temper? Well, you see I admit it! Come back, lover, and I'll be good, I promise."

He had never seen her so warm, so inviting. Perhaps she had been drinking before he arrived; otherwise she might not have been able to humble herself. And it began to seem to him, as he strolled across the room to replenish his glass, knowing he had plenty of time to answer her, that it might be fun to be once more in bed with this large, splendid creature and to know that her hard nipples and tossing bare limbs depended more on his organ than on her own forensic triumph. And didn't he need it? Hadn't there been enough humiliation, private and public?

"I think you may have a point."

She jumped up. "Then what are you waiting for?"

The image in his mind, as he took her in his arms in her bed, was of the naughty little boy taking a vigorous revenge on the lady teacher. And then the image of Anita's shaking shoulders interfered, and he knew the bliss would fade away and with it his manhood, and there would be nothing, nothing at all. He tried desperately to lose himself in the generosity of Chessie's tense embrace, to become a part of her better existence. But he knew it was no use. For all her frantic and prolonged efforts it was no use.

The light by the bed flashed on. She was up and pacing the chamber, tying and tightening the belt on her long black robe.

"Get dressed and go home!"

"Chessie, it's not my fault. After what happened today —"

"I didn't say it was your fault," she interrupted fiercely. "I know when I'm not wanted. Oh, I don't say you don't *want* to want me. You feel obliged to me. You feel sorry for me, damn you. And why shouldn't you? Big, brassy castrator that I am!" Here she actually heaved a sob. "Oh, my God, I'm getting as mushy as the Vogel woman. Get the hell out of here, will you? Get up and get dressed and get out!"

He hurried to comply. As he buckled his belt and pushed his feet into his shoes, he tried once more to assuage her. "I'll call you in the morning. You'll feel better then."

"Don't call me. You and I are through. I prefer abrupt, clean endings. I knew this wasn't going to work. I just hadn't faced it. Well, now I have. Go!"

And he went. In the rainy street, walking home, he was surprised at his own resilience. If he had, in the past months, come to accept the fact that Chessie was right about virtually everything, maybe he could now accept the most humiliating fact of all: that she was right about him. But however humiliating, he at least had his life back — for whatever that was worth.

He found a message on his answering service when he arrived home. It was from Carol Sweeters: "You and Miss Norton should be glad to learn that the doctors have saved Anita Vogel from the overdose she had taken before arriving at the hospital. Their timely action has also saved you both from my charge of moral manslaughter."

12

CAROL went every evening, when he left his office, to see Anita in the hospital. She was calm again, but it was the calmness of detachment, perhaps of indifference. She sat immobile in her bed, her hands resting on the border of the neatly drawn spread, and gazed at him with wide eyes which seemed faintly to question his being there, but more on the ground of the loss of his time than of hers. There was a tepid friendliness in her manner that seemed to accept his status of the person most nearly interested in her fate. And she was surprisingly candid about what she had done.

"Don't worry, it won't happen again. Because the circumstances won't happen again. When Mark denied those questions about the . . ." She turned her eyes to the East River, rolling and turbid, below her window. She seemed to be debating, but more as a matter of taste than of emotional concern, whether she should articulate exactly what it was that Mark had denied. "You see, the whole thing was suddenly . . . well, so public, so crass, so humiliating, that I simply couldn't bear it. I wanted to blot it out, at any cost. But that's over now. I think I'm on top of any feeling of shame."

"There isn't anything to be ashamed of."

"Yes, I see that now. I can even see Mark's point of view. I see that he couldn't admit those things and have any sort of a museum career left. The suit had put him in a position where he had no alternative."

"I wouldn't go that far." Carol had to make an effort to keep the growl out of his tone. "It seems to me that a gentleman always has the alternative of telling the truth."

"But what he'd done was not important enough to merit the whole truth. A kiss? A couple of kisses? Was it really lying to deny anything quite so inconsequential? What would a kiss mean to you, Carol?"

"It would mean a pleasure, anyway. Not a rung in the ladder of my ambition."

"You've always been hard on Mark."

"I can't not be, Anita. The guy's a prick and always will be." As he studied her impassive countenance for a sign of the least reaction, he felt a tiny throb of hope that her troubles might have killed her last bit of feeling for the director. But had they killed everything else? Was it better to have her alive and himself jealous or both dead? In his need to push past this disturbing question he asked abruptly, "What did the doctor say today?"

"He said that if I continued to improve at this rate, I'd be able to go home in another week."

"Home?"

"Well, that's it. I don't really have one, do I? Not where I wouldn't be alone, that is. He doesn't want me to be alone. For a while, anyway."

"How about your mother?"

"I could go there, I suppose. She came in to see me this morning and was very nice about everything. But that seems like another world, Carol. She and I are basically strangers."

"How about Mrs. Pinchet?"

"Oh, she doesn't want me at all!" Anita showed more amusement than resentment at the idea. Indeed, it brought a faint touch of animation to her features. "She's a total lady and offered to put me up at a hotel with a nurse companion. But I couldn't accept anything from her. I know she thinks I blew her case."

"She hasn't said so, I trust."

"She hasn't had to. No, I really haven't decided where I'll go."

"I might be able to sublet Fred Farr's apartment for you. We're sending him to Yucatán for a month."

"But I have no money!"

"What are you talking about? Where's the Speddon trust?"

"The Speddon trust is right where I left it. And where I intend to leave it."

"You don't mean that you've renounced it!"

"Well, I'm not sure I can, can I? But I don't have to accept the income. I can simply let it pile up and one day maybe give it to charity. Don't look so horrified, Carol. That money was given me in a kind of moral trust. In return for my taking care of her things. And look what a mess has been made of that!"

"But that wasn't your fault. It was Miss Speddon's for changing her will. Or you could even say it was mine for not anticipating that Mrs. Pinchet would bring that crazy lawsuit. My idea had been to let the article in *Art in Town* do the job. The trouble with a lawsuit is that if it's lost or even settled, the bad guys get a kind of vindication."

Anita shook her head. "But even if it wasn't my fault, I'm no longer in a position to do the job the legacy was to pay me for."

"It wasn't to pay you for *doing* anything. It was to pay you for what you'd done. For giving three years of your life to Miss Speddon. The obligation was all on her side. And she recognized it, dear old generous soul that she was!"

"Anyway, I'm not going to touch the money."

"But, Anita —"

"Please, Carol."

He gave it up. For the present, at least. There was no point upsetting her unduly. The trust would always be there for a later, more rational mood. And anyway there was something not altogether unattractive to him in her now complete dependency. An idea was taking rapid shape in his mind that filled him with an excitement so intense that he already dreaded the possibility of its extinction.

"Let me ask you something." He paused, taken aback by his own breathlessness. "You know my apartment. It's large, like so many in the old buildings. Constructed before the measly meanness of today's housing. It has three bedrooms. One I've converted into a little library, but it has a day bed and would do perfectly for a nurse companion. I want you to come there, Anita, when you're released from here."

She seemed really moved. She reached over to touch his hand. "Oh, Carol, that's sweet of you. But I couldn't think of moving you out of your apartment."

"You wouldn't have to. I'd stay. I'd stay and do all the marketing and see the cleaning woman was kept up to scratch. I'd get in a cook, and we'd have gourmet meals. Oh, Anita, we'd have fun! And you can't think me such a beast that I'd ever take advantage of the arrangement."

"No, no, I'm not such a silly fool. I know true kindness when I see it. But I can't think how I could justify putting you to such trouble and expense."

"You don't understand. You're always thinking of what you owe people, never of what they owe you. If you come to my apartment, I'll be the one who's in your debt."

"Why, for heaven's sake?"

"Because you'll have given me the chance to make up for what I did to that cat."

For a moment she didn't seem to grasp the reference; then she almost laughed.

"Oh, Carol, that's sweet of you. Maybe I'll have to think it over. Maybe I really will."

She did, in the end, come to his apartment, and for three weeks they enjoyed something like the amiable relationship he had envisioned. Her recovery, however, was rapid, and by the time she was well enough to find a suitable sublet, she was also ready to take back her old job at the museum, which Harold Stein, touched by her collapse, had insisted she be offered as part of the settlement. Anita had hesitated about accepting, but Carol, divining that it would be a way of easing her conscience about the trust, had represented it as her duty.

"Together we can keep an eye on Claverack," he had assured her. "Of course, he loathes you and me and will lose no opportunity to get rid of us, but he won't dare try anything for a while yet."

And so life on Central Park West had begun to repeat its old pattern, for all the world, Carol thought sullenly, as if nothing had happened to any of the principal performers. He seemed to have made no appreciable gain in the affections of the still listless Anita, and he cast a jealous and suspicious eye on her least dealings with Addams.

He had solved the problem of his own relationship with the director by confining it to a strict formality. When they passed in the corridor he would not even nod, and at staff conferences he would address him as "Mr. Director" and restrict his comments to the business at hand. He had no problem with Mr. Claverack, as the latter, since the ugly publicity of the lawsuit, was rarely seen at the museum. He was electing to keep a low profile during the period when management was carrying out what Carol sneeringly described as its "token" compliance with the terms of the Speddon settlement.

One morning, the hated director made an uninvited appearance in the doorway of Carol's office. He looked more than ever like a clean young man on a *Saturday Evening Post* cover, and his small, hovering smile seemed a kind of anticipatory defense to some expected insult. When Carol simply stared back at him, without a greeting, Mark entered the room and closed the door firmly behind him.

"I think we've got to talk, Sweeters."

"About museum business?"

"And our own. To some extent it's the same thing. I mean we're in the same boat. Sidney Claverack's boat."

"That, Mr. Director, is *your* boat, not mine."

"Well, it's true that it's about *not* to be your boat. Unless you and I do something about it. He aims to get rid of you and Vogel. He's cooking up a scheme to have you both offered jobs in the Institute of Pre-Columbian Studies in L.A., where he has a pal on the board. Of course, I told him that Anita would feel duty-bound to stay here and guard Miss Speddon's things. But he's not listening to me these days."

"And what is all this to you, Addams?"

Mark, without answering, sauntered across the room, his hands in his pockets. He paused before the glass case containing the vision serpent. "Incidentally, I've changed my mind about your snake. Keep him if you want."

Carol felt a constriction in his throat. "The gods of the Mayas have no need of favors from the likes of you."

But Mark, without betraying the least resentment, took a seat before Carol's desk. "I know you're always going to hate my guts, Sweeters, but it can still pay us to work together. Believe it or not, I'm on the Speddon side now. I want to see all those commitments carried out. Every one of them. If I told you I'd had a change of heart you'd laugh at me. So I won't tell you that. I'll just tell you I need your help, and you need mine. The appraisals of the pre-Columbian artifacts given the museum by clients of Claverack are in your locked file. I need them."

"Are you ordering me to open that file, Mr. Director?"

"No. I'm simply asking you to. Look here, I won't beat about the bush. I've been checking his clients' appraisals in the other departments. They're all made by the same appraiser, a stooge of Claverack's dealer, and they're all grossly inflated. That's how he got his clients to give things to us. By getting them three times the tax deduction they were entitled to."

Carol watched the director carefully, his heart beating faster as he began to make out the latter's plan.

"I know that."

"And you never thought anything of it?" Mark's astonishment was unfeigned.

"What should I have thought? All I care about is adding to the collection. What's it to me what a donor deducts? They're all tax cheats, anyway."

"But don't you see, if we put our evidence together, we'll have something to hold over Claverack's head?"

"You mean you'd turn him in to the IRS?"

"No, no, no! We'd drop a hint of it, that's all. Just enough to make him think twice about getting rid of people who oppose him on Speddon. I don't see Claverack risking a rap about defrauding Uncle Sam."

"Is that what it would be?"

"Well, wouldn't it?"

"Ask my secretary for the key," Carol said abruptly, "and do as you like." He turned his attention to the memorandum on his desk and pretended to be absorbed in reading it until he heard the director leaving. Alone, he jumped from his chair and darted across the room to stand by the vision serpent.

He must have stood ten minutes staring down at those coils of jade. He tried to keep from blinking. Then he breathed in deeply, as if to suck in some of the mystery that must have settled in the air over the noble asp. The idea that had flashed over the roof of his mind when Addams made his proposal now hardened into a concept of justice as high and straight and gothic as some ancient English court of law. For if the evidence gathered by Addams for purposes of blackmail (and was it anything else?) were delivered to the proper federal authorities, would it be only the wicked Claverack who bit the dust? No, it would be the wicked Addams as well! For what board of trustees would continue in office a director who had betrayed the chairman and brought his institution into public odium and disgrace? Talk about killing two birds with one stone! With one shining piece of glorious green jade!

He had stared so long at the vision serpent that his own vision blurred. He rubbed his eyes impatiently and resumed his gaze. The jet black orbs of the sculpted creature and its strange little beard, like a bib, reassured him. The Mayas had not been a sentimental people. Their emotions had been absolutes, their colors bright and fixed. The east was red for the rising sun; the west, black for the unknown, the uncovered. Hate was always hate.

It had been agreed that he and Anita would celebrate the completion of her first month back on the job with dinner at an Italian restaurant. Its walls were covered with blown-up photographs of old drawings of famous Italian gardens. Water seemed to cascade over their little round corner table; strange monsters of carved stone or marble forming pilasters and cornices grinned at them with a weird friendliness.

"Oh, but Carol, that's wonderful!" she exclaimed when he told her about keeping the vision serpent. "It's really big of Mark, even you must admit."

"He still behaved like an utter shit to you."

"But what does that matter if he means what he told you about the Speddon things?" There was more animation and color in her face than he had seen at any time since her hospitalization. The serpent had not only uncoiled itself; it was ready to strike.

"Do you really think you can trust him? Him and Claverack?"

"Well, Claverack certainly not. But Mark, yes, I think I really can. He seems to have completely changed his attitude. Why keep on with old grudges? Can't you let bygones be bygones?"

"So Young Lochinvar is come out of the west again!"

"Oh, Carol, you're not going to start all that again?"

"Why the shit not?"

And this was to have been the dinner when, had things gone just right, he had contemplated proposing marriage! Of making a fool of himself for the second time! Well, at least he had been spared that. As he sat moodily staring across the table, he remembered with a wince of mortification that he had referred mockingly on that other occasion to Darcy's haughty proposal to Elizabeth in *Pride and Prejudice*. It had to be some kind of a judgment against him for such folly that his situation should now repeat the great Jane's contrived plot. For Darcy, though spurned by Elizabeth, gains her by saving her sister from social disgrace. Had he been actually inspired by some memory of that sentimental tale to turn his apartment into a nursing home for this penniless and ungrateful creature? Had he been hoping to dazzle her with his generosity and detachment? Really, had a man ever made a more egregious ass of himself?

Thoroughly angry now, he resolved grimly to turn the blade in his own wound.

"And to think I was actually thinking of asking you to marry me!"

Her eyes were full of dismay. "Oh, Carol, my dear, dear friend, don't talk that way, please. I'm not ready for anything like that yet. Really not."

He looked at her with baleful suspicion. "And not from Lochinvar either?"

"Not from anybody, silly."

He sighed and picked up his napkin. He supposed it would have to do.

He was to wonder afterwards if he would really have had the guts to go through with it if a Mr. Ackerly of the Internal Revenue Service had not called on him the Monday following for a personal inspection of the vision serpent. For after Carol had gone to Zürich to inspect that sculpture in the auction gallery, he had written to the banker who headed the Friends of the Mayan Collection at the museum to suggest that he buy it for them. The banker had done so, and it was his tax return that was now being audited. His appraiser, however, had been an honest one, obtained by Carol and not by Claverack.

What had thrilled Carol — thrilled even as it chilled him — had been the discovery, at the beginning of the interview, that Mr. Ackerly was not the regular auditor on the case but the head of the department, who had come in the stead of his inferior because, as an amateur collector of Mayan artifacts, he had taken a personal interest in the serpent. The gods of the rivers and meadows of Yucatán had conspired against Carol's rival!

"While I was reviewing the matter, Dr. Sweeters, I thought I'd take the opportunity of going to the museum and inspecting the asp myself. I've never had the pleasure of visiting your institution."

"Well, now, as they say, that you know the way . . ."

"I'll come again, of course. So this is it?" Ackerly stared for several silent moments at the spiraling jade. "What is that coming out of its mouth?"

Carol repressed a smile. The man was indeed an amateur. "That is the head of the person having the hallucination that he is becoming the god represented by the serpent. The Mayas believed in an animate universe, peopled by large numbers of deities. It was important, to be favored by these, for mortals to be in constant touch with them. That is why a noble, or even a monarch, in such a ritual would be costumed as a god, in this case a serpentine one. And by drugs or bloodletting, he would reach a state where he hallucinated that he *was* that god. The artist's job was to commemorate the ritual to instruct posterity how these necessary things were accomplished."

"The serpent god would then do something for the tribe?"

"Presumably."

"Was the visionary then sacrificed?"

"No, no. That fate was reserved for captives. Though undoubtedly some of the bloodletters died as a result of their too-drastic cutting. But it was a happy death. Happier, at any rate, than what probably awaits you and me."

"You sound as if you envied the Mayas, Dr. Sweeters."

"They lived closer to reality than we. They knew things that we don't know. They gave names and shapes to unknown objects; they called them stars and moons and jaguars and monkeys and snakes and people. They brought the universe into their temples and learned to cope with time and death. They were clear and ruthless where we are confused and sentimental."

"But didn't they go in for human sacrifice?"

"Oh, yes, yes."

The auditor coughed as if to indicate that they had gone far enough for him. "And what makes you think, Dr. Sweeters, that this serpent is worth so much more than the taxpayer paid for it in Zürich?"

"Because it was a steal in Zürich! It was I who spotted it and knew what it really was."

"I see. But shouldn't the vision serpent be represented as rampant? Didn't I read that somewhere? This one seems to be totally relaxed. As if it had swallowed something and was digesting it."

"Perhaps a tax auditor." Carol didn't care if he angered him now. He had lost interest in the man and was once more rapt in contemplation of the snake. If sacrifice it called for, was this not the moment? He felt his skin tingling with a delicious, exhilarating sense and closed his eyes tightly. Maybe the serpentine god *was* there! Why not? Wasn't it as likely as anything else in a world so ridiculous as to place its confidence in Claveracks and Addamses? Oh, the joy of it! The joy!

"In *this* case, Mr. Ackerly," he pronounced, "the appraiser was honest."

"You speak as if that were exceptional."

"It is. In the Museum of North America."

Ackerly smiled until he recognized that Carol was not smiling in return. "You sound almost serious, Dr. Sweeters."

"I have never been more serious, Mr. Ackerly. I speak advisedly to a Revenue Service department head. I fully realize that the ordinary auditor would have no interest in any tax return beyond the one he happened to be auditing. He might even close his ears to anything that would mean more work on his part. But you, on the contrary, may be interested to know how many times Uncle Sam has been cheated by donors of this institution."

Ackerly's eyes narrowed; the police dog had scented the cat. "I am very much interested, Dr. Sweeters."

"Let me tell you then about an appraiser called . . ."

If Sidney Claverack and Mark Addams would not slit their own penises, it was fortunate there was a priest to do it for them.

13

ONE OF PETER HEWLETT'S private jokes was that the library in his apartment, which at first glance might have struck an untutored eye as the paneled retreat of a recognizable Park Avenue tycoon, complete with unread sets of classics, duck decoys and nineteenth-century English hunting prints, was actually the ideal from which such banal copies were made. The large carved swan on its own little round Sheraton table was the masterpiece of Elmer Crowell, the Michelangelo of sculpted waterfowl. The books, "armorial," leather-bound in rich, restful-to-the-eyes pinks, greens and yellows, were arranged on the shelves so that every tenth volume faced outwards to display the gilded crest and coat of arms of its royal or noble owner. The paneling was of dark mahogany; the ceiling of white plaster carved with Tudor roses and drawbridges, and over the Jacobean mantelpiece hung a Ben Marshall painting of a master of fox-hounds on foot, surrounded by his barking canines.

But there were times when Peter wondered whether the joke might not be on him. If, in a household of females, he liked to think that he maintained a kind of control by his own quick temper, quickly appeased, and that he was obeyed, not so much that his womenfolk respected the brilliance of his intellect as that they deemed him at heart a sentimental old darling, he still could not escape little reminders that his wife and daughters, like those barking hounds, might at any moment turn on their master despite his long whip and rend his scarlet coat to shreds. What would his Crowell or even books bearing the arms of France quartered with Austria do for him in such an eventuality?

And such an event seemed to loom on the morning when Augusta came into the room with a pad and pencil, like a secretary ready for dictation. Yet the moment she sat down, it was clear who would be dictating. Augusta never intruded on his sanctuary unless the matter was serious, and then she did not knock.

"I've made a list of things for you to check on while I'm gone. There's very little, really. The household pretty well runs itself."

He elected not to look surprised, if only to defeat her expectation. "I hope you have a good trip."

"Oh, I expect to have a fine trip. The Caribbean should be lovely in March."

"Is it a cruise?"

"Yes. On the *Excalibur*. Three weeks. Nassau, Jamaica, Antigua."

"You're going alone?"

"Oh, no. Sadie May is going with me. And two friends of hers, also widows."

" 'Also' like Sadie? Or 'also' like you?"

"Like Sadie, of course." Augusta did not acknowledge his sarcasm.

"But I thought women lucky enough to have hung on to their consorts did not have to join up with deprived ones."

"They don't act deprived. They're less gloomy, anyway, than those with husbands in wheelchairs."

"Oh, come off it, Augusta. How many of my contemporaries are in wheelchairs?"

"I was speaking metaphorically. Men don't usually age as well as women."

"In what way am I aging less well than you? I speak of the mentality, of course. There's no competing with that perfect skin and figure of yours."

Augusta took no more notice of his gallantry than she had of his sarcasm. "Of course there's nothing wrong with your mind, Peter. There never has been, and I rather doubt there ever will be. But you've always had a streak of selfishness, and now it's more than a streak. At the rate you're going, if you don't watch out, it may swallow you up."

Her voice had sharpened in tone. The issue was now joined. But he found that he was trembling with pain and anger.

"We never object to a general state in the morals of our nearest and dearest. It is always to a particular blemish. How then have I been selfish to you, my dear?"

"It's not just to me. It's to the girls and to our grandchildren. All you care about these days is your new gallery at the museum."

"Ah, the gallery, of course, the new gallery. You have it in for me because of my pictures. But what's new about that? Haven't you, basically, always? Even when you were helping me to choose them? You've always been jealous of my collection, Augusta. I suppose any wife would be."

"Don't try to put me off with psychiatric bromides. You know perfectly well that what I mind is not your buying pictures but your giving them all away and depriving your family of their rightful inheritance."

"But Julia told me that if I gave them away in my lifetime you'd have no objection! She said your only worry would be if you found yourself saddled with a right of election against my will. Which you won't be, because I'm leaving you your full intestate share."

"You mean my share of what's left after the big plums have been plucked. Thank you very much. Julia thinks she knows you and me down to the last nut and bolt. It's almost insulting of her, and certainly condescending. What's more, it's not true. I'm not such a fool as you and she suppose. The last thing that concerns me in all this is my duty. It's yours I'm thinking of. Your duty to the children you brought into this world."

"You think it's my duty to keep everything so that I may leave them everything? And give nothing away?"

"No. I think it's your duty to leave them their proper share. And I think that if you and I sat down to discuss the matter calmly and rationally, you'd find that we'd probably agree as to what that share would be. After all, you're not a communist or socialist. If you were, if you really and truly believed that you ought to give everything to the state, I wouldn't so much mind. But you're no such thing. You're a dyed-in-the-wool capitalist, and you know in your heart that you're doing a wrong thing to your children. Well, don't do it!"

"Augusta, if I give you my word of honor that each of our daughters is going to be very well off —"

"What good is your word of honor in a case like this? How can I possibly be sure of what you say unless I have all the facts and figures? And how do we know what 'well off' will be by the time you come to die? Suppose Julia, for example, wants to become a collector? Suppose she wants to support a museum, like you? Shouldn't she have the same right to an inheritance that you did? What would your collection have been without your father's fortune? And don't give me that tommyrot about your having bought it all for a song, because you didn't. You made some good bargains, surely. But you've also paid some tidy sums, sometimes too much. Remember all the money you sank into that Mexican muralist —"

"Oh, Augusta, please!" His temples were throbbing, and he

reached up to feel his sweat. My heart, he thought with sudden panic. He had to remember his heart. Resolving to keep calm, he confined his expression to a lugubrious stare. "And so you have decided to punish me by leaving me, is that it? You will sail away with Sadie May and enjoy yourself in the company of the fortunate widows? Perhaps you won't come home at all. At least until you find yourself also translated to that happy state. I daresay it will be at no very distant date."

"Oh, Peter, don't be an ass!" Augusta actually stamped her foot, a rare gesture with her. "You're just trying to make a tragedy out of your own pettiness. In a melodrama everything gets a pretty costume, doesn't it? Even plain, ordinary, common-or-garden selfishness gets dressed up. Well, I won't put up with it. You can take off that costume and see yourself as your family see you. And to give you time to do that, I'm going off on my cruise. For I can be selfish, too!"

Peter, in the days after she had sailed, found himself in a sorry state of depression. If he could have condemned her attitude as arbitrary and unreasonable, he might have been able to continue to dramatize his resentment, blowing it up to a stature that would almost have made up for his desertion and isolation. But so long as an occasional ray of light as to the horrid possibility of her judgment being correct stabbed into the darkness of his wounded self-esteem, he was helpless against the mood.

"And why do I care so much?" he asked himself aloud, squinting bleakly at his own foolish image in the shaving mirror. "The woman has simply no conception of what it means to be married to one of the great collectors of our time!"

And then he looked around with a nervous twitch to be sure the bathroom door was closed and that Annie the chambermaid wasn't making his bed. If anyone were to hear his raving!

His only comfort was his daily visit to the museum, where he would spend an hour with Mark Addams going over the plans for the Hewlett gallery. He had rapidly become devoted to this cheerful, compliant young man, whom he had previously considered too much Claverack's protégé to be anyone else's. But since the lawsuit Sidney had begun to express doubts about his former favorite, and this had immediately predisposed Peter in favor of Addams. For Peter had never quite trusted the chairman. Sidney was undeniably useful, generous, perhaps even indispensable to the institution, but Peter still kept a wary eye on him. Perhaps it was simply that he felt that Sidney handled Peter Hewlett too well.

One morning, as he was about to leave Mark's office, it occurred to him that the usually high-spirited director had seemed a bit tired and disconsolate, and he recalled not only the trouble that a critical chairman might be giving him, but something he had heard from the elegant, elderly Miss Tillinghast, curator of silver, with whom he often paused to exchange daily gossip, about a breakup between Addams and his lawyer girl friend. Perhaps the young man was worried and temporarily at loose ends. He turned back from the door.

"I'm a cruise widower for the next two weeks, Mark. If by any chance you're free this evening and looking for a good meal, I think I can do pretty well for you at the Patroons Club. You can always 'go on' if you have what is known as a 'late date.' "

"Why, I'd love that, sir! And don't worry about late dates. The way I feel right now, I'm through with the sex for good."

"For good's a long time."

"Well, for a long time, then."

In the huge, high-ceilinged, almost empty dining room, under the School-of-Tiepolo fresco, with the bad, dark portraits of deceased club presidents looking down at them, Mark and Peter dined lengthily and well. They had had two cocktails apiece at the bar; they had drunk a bottle of white wine and were now drinking one of red; and they had become very pleasantly congenial. Augusta in her distant vessel, descending with a swarm of widows on the crammed marts of Caribbean villages, seemed comfortably remote.

Mark was already calling him Peter, and they were actually discussing the former's relationship with the lawyer lady. The younger man was being as frank as if Peter had been a college crony.

"The trouble with Chessie and me was that we were rivals as well as lovers. She's full of sex antagonism. Of course that can sometimes be sexy — Theseus overcoming the Amazon. It can make screwing a livelier business, if it's not carried too far."

Peter felt his throat constrict. This invitation into the scene of the younger man's sporty bedroom was almost too much. He thought of Augusta's passive response to his own fumbling love-making in the years before even that had ceased.

"Our real trouble began during the trial. It gave Chessie too much of an advantage over me. There I was, cutting a sad and sorry figure, and there she was, the blazing righteous advocate. And afterwards, it was as if Shylock was expected to make love to a victorious Portia, though maybe the old boy would have liked that. But not this cat. I knew I wasn't going to make the grade, but like an ass I tried anyway. And Chessie's reaction was horrendous. She couldn't imagine, at least in her psyche, that she wasn't being spurned, even humiliated. It drove her right up the wall."

"But surely you could explain that." Peter feared that his eyes might be bulging as he mentally re-created the scene. "Even if at the moment she was too excited, wouldn't she feel differently in the morning?"

"But there wasn't any morning; that's just the point. She kicked me right out of her apartment. She said all was over between us."

"And that was that? That was final?"

"Not quite. Unfortunately. There were two other occasions when we got together again. You can imagine what happened.

I was so anxious not to have a repeat of those tantrums that I funked it each time. You can't make love with a pistol to your head. At least I can't. And the last time it happened I got sore myself. If she preferred indulging a nasty temper over trying to work things out rationally, she could do so, and to hell with her!"

Peter noted the sudden thin line of Mark's lips, which made him now look his age, in his thirties, not his twenties. The boy wonder had ceased to be a boy.

"But you implied that she couldn't help it. That her sense of rejection was not a thing she could control."

"Oh, that may be true enough. She's probably suffering from not having been loved sufficiently by her parents. Or by her adored brother. He killed himself. I suppose there's no harsher rejection than suicide. Yes, I can see it. She fortifies herself against being unloved and hence unlovable by taking up women's causes and becoming a fighting trial lawyer. But then I come along to slip through the fortifications and take the citadel by surprise. And once she's exposed herself, once she's betrayed her secret weakness, I spit on her, so to speak. 'Ah, so *that's* what you've been hiding,' she imagines me crowing. 'Your essential unlovableness!' "

"But, Mark, if you can see all that so clearly, surely you and she can talk it out? Not in the bedroom, perhaps, but, say, at the lunch table?"

"It's possible. But the truth is, it makes sex too clinical for me. I know people prate about understanding and sympathy and couples going together to shrinks, and I don't say it never works. But sex has always come easily to me — until Chessie, at least — and I don't propose to waste my life with someone who makes heavy weather of it. Let Chessie find her own storm partner. Let them enjoy the rumpus they make of a simple thing. As for myself, I'm through with tense Vogels and erupting Nortons. Give me a girl who can love a good roll in the hay and laugh off a punk one. I sometimes wonder if the old puritanism we thought we'd kicked out of morals hasn't gone underground and come back to plague us in the sexual act."

"People have to be serious about something. I've made my god out of art. I suppose the less fortunate may have to make theirs out of screwing."

"Is it a sin to want to enjoy a little peace and quiet with a woman?"

Peter could not help reflecting that he had not perhaps been just to Augusta. She had always been so patiently uncritical of performances on his part that must have been pallid versions of what this finely knit fellow, for all his modesty, was capable of. Suppose he, Peter, had married a Chessie instead of an Augusta! "Good heavens, no!" he answered Mark's question. "There must be plenty of young women glad to offer you that."

"Well, let's drink to it." Mark raised his glass of red wine. "It's really swell of you to let me rattle on like this. I could never talk to my father about these things."

His father! The term cast a chill. But what other relationship indeed was possible? You old fool, Peter Hewlett, he snarled to himself; take what's offered you and be grateful! "If we're going to drink toasts, I think we'd better have some champagne." And he raised a hand to beckon a waiter.

When the Moët-Chandon was uncorked, Peter changed the subject to one that seemed to offer more common ground. "At any rate, you have your work at the museum. That must be your solace until Miss — or Ms. — Right comes along."

Mark seemed immediately disposed to be equally confidential in this field. "Well, that's the great thing, of course. Though it's sometimes a bit difficult to match the term 'solace' with the kind of isolation that's imposed on me there."

"Isolation? You mean the director is held in such awe?"

"On the contrary. The director is held in such disesteem."

"But why on earth should that be? Do you mean they're all jealous of you?"

"They may be that indeed, but it has nothing to do with their low opinion of me. Surely, Peter, you know that I'm generally regarded as Claverack's sidekick? They think he put me up to what I did in the Speddon affair. And they're right, too. He did."

Mark's gray-green eyes, intent now upon his host, took on a look of what seemed almost defiance.

"But, my dear fellow, surely your giving Miss Vogel back her old job — and her being willing to take it — must have quieted people down on that score."

"Not really. I guess they figure it's some kind of tricky ploy. Anita herself has been nice enough, and her friend Carol Sweeters at least talks to me now, but I can never feel sure of him. He's as slippery as an eel. You can't tell where to have him."

"I know. That smile. And those ghastly compliments! I always feel that he's really insulting me. But what strikes me as curious in your situation, my candid friend — if I may be equally candid — is that Claverack himself does not seem to regard you in the same light that you say the staff do. Far from considering you his sidekick, I'm under the distinct impression that he wonders whether you're not entirely too independent of the sacred trustees. And in particular of the sacred chairman."

Mark's immediate broad smile seemed, charmingly, to accept the worst. "Exactly. You might say that I've slipped between two stools. A toady to the staff and a rebel to the board. Oh, Peter, if only you were in Claverack's place! I think we'd get on wonderfully. Why don't they rotate the job of chairman? They do in some museums."

Peter had a sudden dazzling vision of their working together, the wise old Roman emperor leaning on the strong shoulder of his adopted successor, the perfect union of sagacity with adventure, of experience with innovation, of an old man's love with a young man's . . . well, affection. Yes, surely he could call it that!

"Well, of course it's my fault. I've always tended to avoid administrative work, and there was Sidney just dying to take it off my hands. Perhaps he has had the job long enough. We'll see." Peter gazed now complacently into the golden mist of his glass. "Tell me something, Mark. So long as you are fancy free at the moment, how would you like to come down this weekend to Long Island? You've never had a proper look at the pictures there. Come on down — we'll be all alone. Inez is away, I believe, and her children are in their own wing. We'll eat well and drink well and revel in beautiful things!"

It worked out just as Peter had hoped, at least on Friday night and Saturday. Mark showed no interest in having any company but his host's, and he roamed with him through the treasure-laden rooms, between succulent meals, with long appreciative pauses before each work of art. Even when, on Saturday afternoon, he organized a softball game for Inez's children and some of their friends, Peter felt gratifyingly included, for Mark insisted that he act as umpire and feigned a jocular but still convincing outrage whenever a youngster had the nerve to challenge the old boy's ruling. The house came alive under Mark's enthusiasm as it never had under Augusta's silent and efficient management.

Only once was Peter upset by anything his guest said, and that was when, standing before the Gauguin of the Pont-Aven period, a shimmering green summer landscape with yellow wheat and three small, white-capped Breton women, he exclaimed: "You know, Peter, anything so beautiful begins to quell my doubts about putting European art in a museum dedicated to another continent. After all, beauty is beauty, and there isn't so much of it around that we can afford to be too fussy about periods and geographies. So long as I can see *that* in a museum, am I going to care that some people might think it really belonged in the Met or the National Gallery?"

So Mark had doubts. Well, of course, he would have. Peter

should have known that. And now Mark was going to have to get over those doubts; that was all.

What was much worse — oh, very much worse — was Inez's arrival on Saturday night in time for dinner. She had been staying with her sister Doris in Greenwich, a visit that always put her in a bad mood, as Doris invariably managed to insinuate the superior position of the younger and still married sibling to the older divorced one. And then, too, Doris's husband was rich and successful, and Inez had to be partially supported by her parents. But when Inez saw Mark, of whose bachelor status and temporary freedom from romantic entanglement she had evidently been somehow apprised, she became as soft and pliant and rolling-eyed as a cat in heat. She paid scant attention to her father and directed every remark to the affable but (Peter prayed) not unduly impressed director.

As the conversation developed, it became uncomfortably apparent that Inez was quite prepared to make a bonfire of her old man to warm even the fingertips of this potential admirer.

"I can just imagine what a dull weekend you two must have been having, cooped up here alone. Really, Dad, couldn't you have arranged something better for poor Mark? A game of golf or tennis at Piping Rock? Or had some neighbors over for a drink? But no, I can see what he's been exposed to." Here she winked conspiratorially at Mark. "Lectures, lectures and then more lectures about all the art in the house. My, my. How are your tactile values, Mark? In good significant form?"

Peter would not have believed that even Inez could be so odious. Mark, he had to acknowledge, responded with great tact. He managed to smile at her jokes, all meanly pointed at her father, treating them as if they were the friendly jibes of a fundamentally adoring daughter, and at the same time to imply, by glancing with a little nod at his host, that any implication that the weekend had not been the greatest fun was patently absurd.

"I'm not a great one, Inez, for club sports. That softball game with your kids was just fine for me. The rest of the time I was more than happy to relax and bask in this beautiful atmosphere. Your father's been the deprived one. He's probably been pining to get out on the golf course."

"Oh, Daddy doesn't play golf. He doesn't play anything, really. His idea of exercise is to stroll along the bay and yack about Monet and Manet. But if you'd like, I can give you a bit of a change after dinner. Betty and Al Herrick are having a party down the road. I told them I didn't know when I'd be getting in from Greenwich, so they said to come over any time. How about it?"

"What do you think, Peter?"

"Oh, Daddy hates going out after dinner. Besides, there won't be anyone his age there."

"Well, thanks very much, but I think I'll stay here with him."

"You don't have to, you know. He always likes to go to bed early."

Peter was beside himself. Not only did he resent Inez's active effort to appropriate his guest; he was upset by the suspicion that Mark really wanted to go. The Herricks were well known as party givers; the atmosphere would be bright and festive. He might even find a mate, even Inez, God forbid! But the one thing Peter knew he must not let himself be was the curmudgeon who stands between youth and gaiety. And he had too much sense to taint the picture that he hoped he had created in Mark's mind of the old epicure reigning in his temple of art with the less lovely image of the old fogy unwanted at the younger party. Could he not just hear the diplomatic Betty Herrick's too-gracious greeting: "Oh, Inez, darling, what a sweetie pie you are to have brought your wonderful father! I wouldn't have dared ask him to this philistine affair. And now I shall drag him into a corner and have him all to myself. For I put everyone on notice that I entertain a clandestine passion for Mr. Hewlett!"

"No, Mark, you must go. I insist. Inez is quite right. I like to turn in very early."

Mark allowed himself to be taken off to the Herricks' immediately after dinner, and Peter, too vexed to be able to read in bed, took two sleeping pills that he might not hear the crunch of wheels on the gravel below his window and know how late they came in.

However late it had been, Mark was down in time to breakfast with him on Sunday morning. Gratifyingly, he made no reference to the party but started at once on a discussion of the Manet in the dining room.

"I was thinking, when I woke up, that I'd found just the place for it in your new gallery —"

Inez, who never rose till lunch time on Sundays, came in at this point and took her seat.

"Heavens, what brings you down so early?" Peter asked, a bit cattily. "I thought only a fire alarm would get you out of the sack before noon."

Inez's glance at her father was baleful. "I thought I'd better rescue Mark from the early morning lecture. I'll bet you're on the subject of the museum already."

"If we are, it's because Mark brought it up."

"Did he? Then you have him obsessed." Angered perhaps that Mark should look so fresh, in contrast to her own puffed cheek pouches and dark undereyes, infallible evidence of her late hours and alcoholic consumption, she proceeded now to challenge her parent on his own ground. She turned to Mark. "I suppose you were talking about Daddy's new gallery. Or is it galleries, by now? I know it's heresy to say it, but how far can you really go along with his little game of giving every artist abroad some kind of Western ticket to fit him into a museum supposedly dedicated to North America? The games people play to cram things into categories where they don't belong! Is Henry James a Yank or a limey? Did that hysterical last-minute change of citizenship really give him to His Britannic Majesty?

And what about T. S. Eliot? And John Sargent? And Arshile Gorky and Rothko and de Kooning and all the rest? And Einstein? God bless America! A few more pogroms abroad, and Daddy can stick all the world into your museum!"

Peter put down his napkin and left the breakfast table. He thought it almost safe to abandon Mark to a woman making herself quite so unattractive.

In the back seat of the old Cadillac limousine, returning to the city that afternoon, Mark revealed to Peter that Inez had asked him down for the following weekend.

"I hope you're coming," Peter responded in a tone that committed him to nothing.

"As a matter of fact, I'm not. I told her I had a heavy work schedule. I trust you don't mind, sir."

The "sir" still occasionally slipped out. Peter let it pass. "I don't mind at all, dear boy. As a matter of fact, I shall be staying in town myself next weekend."

Delighted with this victory over Inez, he decided to push his luck, and he invited Mark, when they arrived in town, to dine with him a second time at the Patroons. His weekend house guest obviously had no excuse, and he seemed willing to accept; Peter enjoyed a sense of exhilaration when he found himself once again with his young friend in the huge dining hall under the ceiling of naked nymphs, who were safely made only of paint.

"You know, Mark, there *is* something to be said for men's clubs. It may be heresy to utter the words, at least in liberal circles, but I impenitently maintain that the sexes have something to gain from occasional segregation. It's not really so much a case of excluding women as it is of excluding sex. Of having some place where social relations can be conducted without the intrusion of physical attractions."

Mark looked around at the bad portraits of the old men and smiled. "What about homosexuals? Wouldn't you have to keep them out too?"

"Most emphatically! Except those who stayed firmly in the closet. I'd have no pinching at my bar."

"When you put out to sea? I used to have arguments on that subject with my friend Chessie. She claimed that no close human relationship was free from all degree of sexual attraction. You might not be conscious of it, but there it was."

"Even between you and me?" Peter chuckled as if he had cited some boundary mark of fleshlessness. But he was sorry as soon as he had said it. It was only too evident, even to his reluctant and prudish imagination, that in his desire to enfold this handsome young man in what he liked to think were paternal arms, all kinds of homoerotic urgings might lurk. He felt no great need to worry about this, because he was perfectly aware that nothing short of a mind-numbing stroke would ever keep him from behaving like a gentleman. It was nonetheless the better part of valor not to go skipping around on those slippery borders. "Well, I suppose we're all monsters in our ids. But I still think men have something to offer men, and women no doubt women, in occasional isolation from the other sex."

"I don't think any but fanatical women's libbers would give you much of an argument on that. It's just the doing business in clubs that they don't want to be kept out of."

"But we don't do business at the Patroons!"

"Oh, Peter, how can you say that? You do it all the time. You're doing it tonight. Isn't the museum your real business?"

"Then everything's business."

"Isn't that what Marley's ghost said? 'Mankind was my business'!"

"But not womankind."

This was a subject on which Peter could wax very hot, but he was sure that there was no subject over which it was worth his while to get angry at Mark.

The next morning he telephoned Inez to tell her that Mark was not coming down the following weekend. He must have allowed some note of satisfaction to creep into his tone, but even so he was hardly prepared for the poisoned arrow that she now struck into his heart.

"Did you talk him out of it?"

"Why should I have done that? I told him that I wouldn't be there myself."

"And why did you do that?"

"Because I won't!"

"Isn't that a rather sudden change of plans?"

"Really, Inez, what are you getting at?"

"Simply that the poor young man, who is after all a kind of dependent of yours, couldn't very well agree to come to your house when he'd been coldly informed that you wouldn't be there."

"Coldly? I wasn't cold."

"Do you think I can't imagine how you said it?"

"Inez, I repeat. What the hell are you getting at?"

"Watch out, Daddy. We don't want you turning into a dirty old man who wants the handsome young director all to himself."

Even in the red wrath that made the room around him seem to crackle, he was still aware that a last-minute moderation was making Inez try feebly to turn her murderous onslaught into the appearance of a bad joke. And then a kind of panic seized him. Was he really known that way? Did people actually smirk as they said such things about him? At last he emitted an audible growl of anger and hate. "Don't be more of a bitch than God made you."

Her scream deafened him, and he dropped the telephone on the desk. As his hearing returned, he gazed at the instrument in dismay. He could make out a babbling and the words "unnatural father" and "beast" and then a great hullabaloo of tears and threats of leaving the house with all her brood. With a deep sigh of recognition at the irreparable damage he might have done, he put the instrument back in its cradle.

. . .

Julia, the following evening, was dining with him and Mark at the French restaurant Oise, amid scarlet draperies and eighteenth-century portraits that were actually not copies. Peter had deliberately selected the place as the most expensive in town to reward Julia for her diplomacy that same day in patching up a truce with the alienated Inez. For it had come over Peter in a horrible moment that if Augusta should return to find Inez and her family gone, in addition to all the business of the gifts and the gallery, she might really walk out on him for good.

Julia had never seemed brighter nor more brilliant, and she and Mark, studying their menus and prices, were having a congenial time making up, as he had urged them, the most expensive meal that money could buy and then blandly ordering it. They seemed in the shortest possible time to have established a happy rapport and one that entirely included him. Peter beamed at both of them. How did Julia do it?

As the meal progressed, she turned from the subject of food and wines to the topic that Inez had despised.

"I've heard that your forte is handling collectors, Mark. Perhaps because you understand that the collector himself is a kind of artist. I used to play a game of trying to piece together the great collectors from their collections. With J. P. Morgan it was obviously magnificence. All the gaudy courts of old Europe glitter in his things. With Frick it was to create an illustrated history of art. With Mrs. Havemeyer . . . no, I was never sure what Mrs. Havemeyer was after. Her El Greco cardinal put me off. Why a cruel and bigoted grand inquisitor? And then I read somewhere that the subject wasn't Guevara at all, but some other, lovable old cardinal who had collected rare books and manuscripts."

"And she wouldn't have bought him had she known that?" Mark asked.

"I really think she might not have. Is that absurd? I don't know why I should associate poor Mrs. Havemeyer with the inquisitor, and yet I felt he was somehow a key."

"What about your father?"

"Oh, Daddy . . . well." She fixed a long, affectionate gaze on Peter. "Daddy likes to capture the world in little perfect slices and tuck it away in jars. Each picture must be a whole in itself. His El Greco, the *Auto-da-Fé,* is just that and only that, as his crucifixions are only crucifixions. And his landscapes are always detached and independent as the rest of the geography."

"Which is why he's so passionate about Cezanne? And maybe why there are no seascapes?"

"That's it! One can't look at seascapes without thinking of more sea. And I'll go a step further. It may be why there are no abstracts."

"Because they can't be separated from infinity?"

"And infinity terrifies me!" Peter broke in now with delight. "Oh, you two read me like a book."

Julia reached for his hand resting on the table. "And it's a very good book."

"A classic," Mark agreed.

"Well, that calls for champagne! Mark will think I'm always ordering champagne. Why not?"

When he went back to his apartment that night, Peter was thoroughly relieved and happy. He decided that he had never had a more wonderful evening in his whole life. But the trouble with wonderful evenings was the speed with which they were over. There was only one thing that would make this one last forever.

He turned on the light by his bed and called Julia's number.

"Are you still up?"

"Daddy, you know I'm a night owl. What's up?"

"Are you alone?"

"You mean did I lure your director up here with lascivious intent? No, I'm alone, however shameful to admit."

"Julia, dear. You've got to marry him."

"Daddy! Are you drunk?"

"I was never soberer. You're both the right age. You both have the right tastes and temperaments. And you're both divine human beings. To me, anyway. He's fancy free, and I believe you are, too. Oh, darling, grab him, give me a son-in-law, and I'll give you my whole damn collection!"

"You *are* drunk. Go to bed."

"I'm in bed."

"Go to sleep, then."

"Just promise me you'll think about it. That's all I ask."

"Daddy, for God's sake!"

"Only think about it. Is that so much to ask?"

"All right, I'll think about it. Now good night!"

"Bless you, my child. Bless you."

And without even seeking to justify his absurd sense of optimism, he switched off his light and fell almost at once into a black sleep.

14

MARK, in the first weeks of his affair with Julia, found the exuberance of his new happiness tempered with a peculiar recurring suspicion that it was somehow unreal. He would try to reason this away by reminding himself that it might have arisen simply from the contrast that his social difficulties with the staff of the museum offered to the bright merriment that Julia had brought to his extra-office life. He had never before had that boy's sense of "School's out!" in leaving his work. He had always been pleasantly excited by the daily routine, even in his public relations days; and indeed in his Chessie period there had been times when pleasure had seemed at least as arduous as toil. But Julia had a way of making everything seem fun. There was a lightness, even in her most serious moments, that put him in mind of the heroines of Shakespearean comedy, Viola and Rosalind and Imogen. She could be funny when she was indignant; her eyes seemed to laugh when she pulled herself up straight.

When his mother, a still pretty, plump but very sober widow, trying to conceal her considerable zest for life behind the transparent veil of her New England propriety, and his obese and loquacious unmarried sister came down from Maine for a weekend in the wicked city, Julia, as their guide, had been generous enough to help them enjoy the sights of Manhattan without so much as a hint that they reconsider their complacent conviction that home had to be the better place.

On the last day of their visit, when he and Julia had called at the hotel to say goodbye, his mother took advantage of his sister's trip to the desk to pay the bill, to ask: "I suppose you two are keeping house together?" This was accompanied by a shrewd glance and a nod to indicate that even in Augusta they kept abreast of the sexual revolution.

"Mark hasn't moved in with me, if that's what you mean, Mrs. Addams. Nor I with him. But I shan't deny we are lovers. Does that seem very wrong to you?"

"Well, of course, it wasn't done in my day. Leastwise, not so anyone knew it. But I reckon there's no great harm in it, if it's generally tolerated. Does your ma approve?"

Julia appeared to reflect. "I don't really know if Mother knows. She rarely talks about personal things. But I suppose Daddy must have told her. And *he* certainly approves."

"He doesn't think you and Mark ought to get hitched?"

Julia's laugh was clear and spontaneous. "As a matter of fact he does. You know, Mrs. Addams, a girl has a double role to play these days. In the past, when a young man came from Down East to the big city, the sleek, sophisticated woman he took up with was supposed to get the hayseeds out of his hair and polish up his manners for the dear little girl next door he would soon go home to marry. But now she has to be both."

"So you think you're polishing up my manners, Julia?"

"Well, haven't I? Mrs. Addams, I appeal to you!"

Mark's mother, thoroughly amused now, glanced from one to the other. "Hang on to this girl, Mark."

This was as near as he and Julia had come to a serious discussion of marriage. He didn't introduce the topic again, but he was glad it had come up. It distilled a small golden glow to the hours they were apart. He did, however, refer again to the supposed role of the city girl.

"So you think you've smoothed my rough corners? The folks back home wouldn't know me now?"

"Did they ever? Who knows what abysses lurk behind those smiling green eyes?"

Was she entirely joking? How much had her father told her about the lawsuit? They had talked around the subject, but Mark had been less than candid. He had promised her that the Mark Addams of that episode was no more, and she had seemed to accept this, but then she was deep. And was it true? Wasn't he Johnny-on-the-make again? If he, the kid from the country, the penniless director of a small museum, should wed the rich and socially prominent daughter of a principal trustee, would anyone in the world of cultural institutions believe for a minute that he had been motivated by love alone? Couldn't he just hear Carol Sweeters chuckling, as he leaned over Anita's desk to show her the announcement of the engagement in the *New York Times*, "I see your friend Mark's got his ass in a tub of butter."

He had his first inkling that some of the sense of unreality that made up in part both the delight and the bewilderment of the affair might be caused by something in her past, with which she had not fully come to grips, at a cocktail party she took him to. There had been a number of these; she introduced him easily into the circle of her friends and clients, and seemed to know at once, despite his good party manners, just who bored him and who didn't. Nor did she embarrass him by too promptly giving in to his occasional impatience. If the bore happened to be a lady who was about to redecorate an apartment, she would tell him firmly that she expected him to "work." At this particular party he found himself talking to one Ellen Lanier.

She was a type he had learned to recognize in Julia's world: the plain, stout, plain-spoken woman with such utter confidence in her social position as to feel no need of feminine charm or even, for that matter, of aught but the slimmest good manners. He was not surprised, therefore, after she had invitingly patted the empty seat on the sofa beside her, to be asked to hand over the keys to his private life.

"I'm talking to you as one of Julia's oldest friends. I think she's been hiding you from me. Why should she do that?"

"Maybe she thinks someone will steal me."

"In that case hadn't she better marry you? Is that in the cards? You're both of age, surely."

He glanced across the room to her equally stout spouse, who was holding a dark drink that certainly interested him more than the chattering women around him, and wondered if he, too, would recommend marriage.

"I guess you'd better ask Julia about that."

"I have, but she won't tell me. All I really want to know is whether you'll be good to her."

"What makes you think I wouldn't?"

"It's nothing about you personally. It's just that I know how terribly hurt she can be. Oh, she doesn't show it, I know. No one could be a cooler cooky, more seemingly self-reliant. But that's a mask. I know because I saw my brother, Drew Ames, hurt her eight years ago. That was when she put on the mask."

"What did he do?"

"He was odious about her father. It was what made her break off their engagement. Drew was kind of a red in those days. You wouldn't know it now. He checked his hammer and sickle after he made his first big deal in Pappy's investment firm. Actually I think he took up socialism just to get Pappy's goat. But the old man was too smart for that. He knew he'd only have to wait for Drew to come round."

"And was Julia a left-winger back then?"

"Julia never had any political opinions that I could make out. But she certainly cared about Drew and his. He was handsome then. Now he's like Joe." She looked across the room at her husband with what struck Mark as a complacent bleakness.

"Drew's trouble was that he had a cruel streak. He still has, I guess, though his wife is too insensitive to feel it. He was always expounding his socialist views in a way to make everyone else feel idle and useless. And he couldn't leave off the subject of Mr. Hewlett."

Mark felt a faint weariness stealing over him, the sure sign of impending disillusionment. He twitched his shoulders to shake it off. Why did people have to find psychological maladjustment in every happy relationship?

"Well, I suppose Peter Hewlett has his vulnerable points."

"Yes, and Drew was merciless about them. He considered Mr. Hewlett the epitome of capitalist hypocrisy because he posed as an art lover. What did he accomplish, Drew used to ask, but enrich crooked dealers by buying their stuff to give away for tax deductions? And he'd say that sort of thing to Mr. Hewlett himself! With a kind of sneering laugh to make it seem like a bad joke."

"Well, no wonder Julia dropped him. Who wouldn't have?"

"But Drew wasn't being entirely malicious. He had a theory that the bond between father and daughter was much too strong and he had to do something to break it."

"He certainly went about it in a strange way."

"Well, that's it. But it doesn't mean he didn't have a point. Julia's always had a thing about her father. There's no question in my mind that she'd have married my brother if he'd left her old man alone. And when she finally turned on Drew, it was with a vengeance! I think she even became a decorator because it was the thing he most despised. Drew used to say decorators were faggots who painted the claws and capped the tusks of the capitalist dragon."

"You make your brother sound charming. I wonder that Julia could have been so taken with him."

"Well, he was really quite sexy, if I say so myself. All the girls thought so. Julia wasn't so far gone on her old man as to be totally immune."

Mark at this debated getting up to walk away. But he found he couldn't. "Why are you telling me this?"

"Because I don't want you to make the same mistake my brother did. Because I think Julia's happiness may depend on you. You seem to be the first guy she's really cared about since Drew. The fact that she won't talk to me about you seems revealing. And if you will take her, so to speak, with her father, you'll find that things may work themselves out."

"What makes you so sure that I can put up with what your brother couldn't?"

"Two things. One, that you already get on so wonderfully with Mr. Hewlett. That, Julia *did* tell me. And second, all the things she can bring you."

"What, that she couldn't have brought your brother?"

"I'll be frank. Money and social position."

"So that's what you think of me." He glanced darkly about the room. "I suppose everyone here thinks the same."

"They don't think any the less of you, if that's what you're afraid of. People in this town believe in getting ahead."

He got up, already almost breathless at what he had decided to say to her. "Thank you for your candor, Mrs. Lanier. I think my feeling for Julia may be just strong enough to survive it."

He found Julia in the next room. As soon as she saw his expression, she divined there was trouble. He could not help admiring the ease with which she at once stood up and made her fluent excuses to the man she had been talking to, who happened to be their host. In the crowded elevator they could not talk; he had to wait for the lobby.

"Let's go to the park."

It was only a block away, and they walked there in silence. In the mild fall weather, amid the stalking, cooing pigeons, they found an empty bench, and he told her what Mrs. Lanier had said.

"I was afraid of something like this the moment she came in. With friends like Ellen, as they say . . ." He was relieved to see that she was not going to minimize it. "Of course, Daddy and I have always been close. Unusually close perhaps. But I really don't see why that has to bother people. I began to understand very early how much he needed love. He's a lonely man, you know, with almost no intimate friends. He had a hateful father who completely dominated his pathetic, broken mother and sister. He led an exquisite bachelor's existence, complete with rare books and bibelots, until he married Mother — rather to everyone's surprise, I gather — in his middle thirties. She was devoted and high-minded, and he was happy for a while with her and us three girls. But then something happened. Mother became more and more remote, retreating into herself. I think she was disappointed that she had not been able to make more of him, that he did not have all the potentiality she had originally expected. Mother is a tremendous idealist, and I'm afraid she finds Daddy at times . . . well, trivial."

He could see that she was trying hard to be fair. The last word had caused her a tremor of discomfort.

"But then they had the collection together."

"For a while. But Mother seemed to lose her interest in it. She used to say she cared about pictures and not collections. I think she actually found collections somehow . . . common." Again that tremor. "Which is why I, to some extent, took her place in helping him. Which, I hasten to add, she never in the least resented. I think it was even a relief. I think she saw that, having had no illusions about Daddy, I could be kinder and more tolerant. Oh, tolerant's not the word. For Daddy *is* in some ways a great man. Doris and Inez could never appreciate him except as a lovable old bear of a pa, but he and I . . . well, we have always understood each other. We each know what the other is thinking without being told. And when a sympathy like that exists between two people, why do the others immediately want to break it up?" Up to this point she had been almost apologetic. Now there was a hint of defiance in her tone. "I sometimes think that marriage is the only intimacy permitted in our society. And look what a mess people make of that!"

"This is all very interesting, my dear, but you don't have to beam those beautiful angry eyes on *me.* I don't in the least object to your wonderful relationship with your father. I only wish I had had one like it with my own. But you haven't even touched on the thing your friend said that upset me."

"You mean about the money and social position?"

"Damn right I mean that."

"I thought that was simply too vulgar to comment on. You've probably discovered that people in what is called 'society' are the most vulgar of all."

"It doesn't bother you that your friends think I'm after your money?"

"Not in the least."

"Would it even bother you if I *were*?"

Her look was one of faint surprise. "I guess I don't know. I never thought of it. I suppose nobody's ever entirely sure what they love someone for. I don't imagine I'd like it if you were *only* after my money. But that's not possible. That wouldn't be my lovely Mark. I don't think it pays to turn over every pebble on the floor of a generous heart. The heart's the thing. And you've got a big one."

She was smiling now; she was begging him not to go on with it. But he was grimly determined to go on with it. "That seems to me just a little too pat. Mrs. Lanier tells me that everyone considers me a gold digger, but that they like gold diggers. Everyone is not always wrong. And isn't the real reason they don't mind my motives that they scent I'm giving value for what I get? That Julia Hewlett needs a husband who will fit in with her father and his collection? And don't I do that to a T?"

She stared down at the pavement. He had really done it now, brute that he was. But when she looked up, it was with a beseeching and not a reproachful expression. "Oh, lover, do you have to spoil everything? Can't you accept happiness? Don't let that ridiculous Ellen or the memory of her horrid brother come between us, for heaven's sake! Supposing we have money and pictures and museums and love and everything in the whole wide world. Can't we enjoy them? How can you expect people *not* to envy us?"

Ah, now he knew he'd have loved her without a penny, and in the very ruins of his bombed-out museum! He took her in his arms and hugged her. "It's getting cold. Where shall we go for dinner?"

"Anywhere that we won't run into the Laniers."

Their affair now entered an intenser phase. Mark found there was no further need to talk of marriage; it seemed almost bound to come. They soon learned that they needed to see each other during the day as well as at night. When she was working on the lobby of a Central Park West apartment house, she would appear at odd moments in his office for a cup of coffee, and he would take her to inspect any new display or renovation. On one such occasion he got Carol Sweeters to take them to see the vision serpent in its new glass case in the Mayan gallery. Julia gazed long and intently at those jade coils before addressing the hovering, smirking curator: "Was it worshiped?"

"Do you mean the sculpture or what it represented?"

"Weren't they the same?"

Carol's smile ceased. "I see what you mean. The man who hallucinated that he was a vision serpent had to become one. And the artist reproducing the process may have undergone something of the same transformation. The Mayas certainly felt that their gods were in daily touch with them."

"So that getting in physical contact with one was not impossible. Like us consuming the host. Eating the body and drinking the blood of Christ."

"Just so." Carol's smile reappeared, but it was now different, the one he offered his equals. "It might also be called the artistic process."

"Because the artist is uniquely privileged to reach behind the veil to reproduce the gods?"

"And other men can only worship his products. Cultivated men, that is. For cultivated men today there are no other gods to worship."

"Are you a cultivated man, Dr. Sweeters?"

"Heaven forbid! I'm a Maya. I worship the god *and* his replica."

"You mean you worship *that*?" Julia's eyes were fixed again on the emerald asp.

"I worship the vision serpent."

As Mark escorted Julia down the corridor to the main entrance hall, he remarked with a touch of impatience, "Sweeters is basically a serious curator. He doesn't always talk such tosh."

She clutched his arm. "Oh, Mark, watch out for that man! He hates you."

"How could you tell?"

"It emanates from him. And did you note that he never looked you in the eye?"

"Anyway, I'm not afraid of his serpent. It's a fake."

"Are you sure?"

"It's hard to be sure of these things. But his very able number two man calls it 'Sweeters's obsession.' "

"Then why do you display it?"

"Because nobody's proved it's a fake. And it's a striking object and keeps Sweeters happy. We can always remove it if some hard evidence turns up."

That afternoon Mark went to the Chrysler Building for his weekly visit to Claverack. The chairman kept an office at the museum, but he exacted this regular pilgrimage as a kind of tribute. Mark, finding him at his most cordial, was at once alerted to danger.

"Good news, my friend. I've had another letter from Laderer, the board chairman of the Institute of Pre-Columbian

Studies in L.A. He'll take both Sweeters and Vogel. I guess we can survive without them, don't you agree?" Here he winked.

"Sweeters is a very good man, sir. One of our best."

"No doubt. But how high would you rate him on loyalty?"

"But that's all over. I really don't see what Sweeters can do to us now."

"I'm afraid you're naïve, my boy. Anyway the die is cast. I've written to my friend on the coast to say that, while we have no wish to lose Dr. Sweeters, if this is a promotion, he has gone as far as he can go here."

"Is that so, sir? Couldn't he become senior curator?"

Claverack's eyes glinted. "Not while I'm on this board."

"I believe the curatorial appointments are supposed to be within the discretion of the director."

"Are you challenging me, Mr. Addams?"

"The issue has not yet arisen."

Mark waited while the chairman debated inwardly his next move. Would he erupt and try to shout his way into making his point? But no, there were other ways of getting rid of uppity directors. When Sidney spoke, he seemed almost relaxed.

"As you say, the question is still moot. And it will never come up if Sweeters accepts this post, which it is obviously in his best interests to do. As it will be in Miss Vogel's."

"Why must you get rid of her as well?"

"Because, man, she is standing between me and the whole development of the museum! She's sitting there like a lugubrious cat, mewing 'Speddon this' and 'Speddon that' every time we stick a thumbtack in a bulletin board. She's got to go, Addams. You must know that as well as I."

Mark felt suddenly sick in the pit of his stomach at the prospect of having to threaten Claverack with the appraisal file. He supposed he had never really believed that it could come to that. And maybe it still wouldn't. "If you mean, sir, do I agree that we should dispose of Miss Vogel so that, when the public has forgotten about Miss Speddon and her will, we may go back to disregarding Miss Speddon's plans, then, no, I do not agree. I believe we are morally bound to carry out the terms of the will that she destroyed, in view of the circumstances of its destruction."

"Morally bound! Since when did public institutions become morally bound by the craven scruples of naïve and replaceable directors?"

"I can only tell you, sir, how I stand. I don't suppose there is much point in our arguing about it. When the time comes that you propose to dismantle any of the Speddon projects that we undertook at the time the suit was settled, I shall make my position clear to the board. And right now I intend to advise Miss Vogel that I consider it her duty to her late patroness to remain at her post. I have little doubt of her agreement."

Claverack sat back in his chair and squinted malevolently at Mark. The tips of his fingers touched and retouched each other. "Well, well, we seem to have grown too big for our director's breeches, haven't we? But maybe not too big to listen to a couple of cooling words of sound advice. Peter Hewlett has some degree of clout in our organization, but perhaps not quite as much as you suppose. And just remember one thing: that when it comes right down to the heart of any matter, trustees tend to side with trustees. Peter and I have understood each other since you were a raw college kid in a hick town up in Maine. And I can promise that you're going to have to do a lot more than screw his daughter to break up an alliance like ours!"

Mark at this could only quit the room without further comment.

15

JULIA sat with her back to her father in a large, bare studio room at the top of the Laidlaw Galleries, contemplating a portrait on an easel. It depicted a lady in a pink velvet dress, in the style of 1900, seated on a divan of gold damask against a dark background in which a vast Chinese vase, blue and white, glimmered. The lady was leaning forward, as if to show a polite interest in what the person — surely a man — standing where the observer was, happened to be saying. Did she quite comprehend him? Perhaps not. But she wanted to make a good impression; one felt she always wanted to make a good impression. She was very pretty, dark-haired, with a high narrow brow and a noble nose, well born, no doubt, and amiable, but of an intellect that could not match her grace. She existed to wear that dress, of such a warm and wonderful pink, a pink one wanted to rub and feel.

"If you were going to buy Sargent, shouldn't you have bought him years ago? In his big slump?"

"Undoubtedly. But I thought he deserved that slump. I

thought, like your mother, that he was slick. Now I'm beginning to rethink him. It's too bad about his prices, but I've a hunch they're going to go even higher."

When Peter studied a painting, he was as intent and still as a cat watching a fluttering bird. He seemed to be actually ingesting it; she could almost imagine the paints beginning to run. It had become a tradition with them that he would call her when he felt the moment of acquisition at hand. There had been times when one of her clients had threatened to interfere, but he had always grumbled, "What does she pay you? I'll double it." These moments in a gallery were the ones when she seemed most to share his collecting genius, when she became an integral part of the process in a way that her mother never had been nor even wished to be. Augusta was always ready with an opinion when asked, and a good one, too, but she was apt to offer it truculently, like an oracle awakened by an importunate truth seeker.

Yet today Julia was unexpectedly conscious of something not unlike her mother's independence. She did not really care for the portrait, except for the pink dress, and there was an element of deference in her father's attitude to it that she found distasteful.

"Do you suppose he tried to paint her just as he saw her?" she asked. "Is she simply mirrored? Or did he mean us to interpret her as I do?"

"How is that?"

Didn't he know? "As a pretty numskull. Adorned by a gold bug of a husband. So that her portrait, like her dress, is simply another example of conspicuous consumption."

"Oh, Sargent saw that. It may be why he gave up 'paughtraits,' as he derisively called them. It's because you can see he's angry with himself for playing the silly society game that the picture has value. 'Is *this* what you really want?' he seems to jeer at his poor sitter. 'Very well, I'll give you a feast!' "

"Until she vomits?"

"No, he stops short of that."

She let him go back to his absorption in the painting. If Drew Ames could see them now! But the golds and pinks of Sargent's fantasy seemed to have survival power. The lady in pink struck her as a caricature of Mona Lisa. Her smile might have mocked the earnestness of a generation of radicals. "Shout your slogans and hurl your bombs, but men will still worship me. Aye, and women too!"

"I've had some rather bad news from the museum." He liked to interrupt his contemplations with extraneous topics. It gave him needed short recesses. "I don't believe Mark knows it yet. Claverack came to see me yesterday. He's under some kind of Treasury investigation about inflated art appraisals. I gather they're claiming he got them for clients who gave paintings to the museum."

"What's going to happen?"

"At worst, they could bring a charge of conspiracy to defraud the government of taxes. I don't know whether the museum staff is involved. Claverack was rather evasive on that point."

"Could he go to jail?"

"Well, of course, he maintains the whole thing's absurd. And I believe these matters are usually settled with fines. But, yes, a jail sentence is always a possibility."

"That would be terrible, wouldn't it?"

"It would be terrible for the museum," he reproached her, frowning. "I know you've never liked Sidney, but even you wouldn't want that. The question is whether the board should call for his resignation pending the outcome of the investigation. I had rather hoped he might offer it, but he didn't."

"I'll bet he didn't. You'd have to take his place, wouldn't you?"

"I imagine so. It should be only temporary. Though something tells me that even if Sidney comes out of this a free man, he won't be clean enough to make the board want him back."

"So it *will* be permanent!" She clapped her hands. "Oh, Daddy, that would be such fun. Mark would love it, and I'd love it, too."

He fixed her now with a long gaze. Even the portrait for the moment seemed forgotten. "If I agree to do this, dearest child, will you agree to do something for me? And for yourself? And for Mark?"

"I know. You want me to marry him. Oh, Daddy, you can be so impossible."

Exasperated, she jumped up to walk to the window. Where was the old wizard now? Who was this Peter Hewlett who slavered over a fashionable portrait and wanted a son-in-law who would speak honeyed words to him and build his gallery? She had a sudden image of the boat that she wanted now recklessly to rock; not a boat, really, a canoe, gliding down a forest stream over still water, she in the middle, her eyes following the bank dreamily, Mark paddling with careful adroit strokes, Peter in the bow, hunched over and peering intently ahead.

"Why is that such an impossible request?" he asked.

"You haven't always been so anxious to marry me off."

"Well, I certainly didn't want to marry you off to Drew."

She stayed at the window, her back to him and the portrait. She recalled with chagrin what she had said to Mark on the park bench about his not accepting happiness. Who was not accepting it now? Why wasn't she welcoming with open arms the wonderful life that seemed to be unfolding before her, a life that was even more neatly and shiningly arranged than the best parlor she had ever decorated, with the museum, enriched by Speddon and rid of Claverack, now under the tandem team of her father and Mark, both loving her and beloved of her? What more could she ask of the gods to make her happy?

Everything! Her life seemed suddenly as wrong as a room that was too perfect. It was artificial, unlived in; it needed inconsistencies, even a clash of colors, perhaps a few odd pictures. Wasn't Mark to have made the difference? And hadn't he done his best to make it? Come now, Julia, she thought to herself, be fair. You know your father's too much of an egoist to match the picture you drew of him for Mark. And you've always known it.

"What are you doing over there, Julia? Aren't you going to help me decide about Mrs. Clyde?"

"No, I've had my fill of Mrs. Clyde. I don't think I'd have liked Mrs. Clyde."

"But, darling, you're not meant to like her. You're meant only to like her portrait."

He had actually said it! For what had she been doing for years but trying to like the portrait she had made of *him*? She had been so obsessed with the idea of bringing order back into her life, after the fiasco of her engagement to Drew, that she had not even minded the banal theory of parental domination with which her friends tried to explain her silly fiction of the sage old priest and the devoted Vestal. Joint worshipers at the altar of art, wasn't that how she had put it? Hadn't it allowed her to have her cake and eat it? To combine the uncluttered life of the dedicated virgin with a rare affair that could be ended without recrimination? Because her supposed preoccupation would be understood by the man who, like as not, was only too willing to have it that way?

But Mark was too good for that. She had thought she could marry Mark and share him with her father. But it had never been a part of her fantasy that her father should like Mark more than he liked her. That made her ridiculous.

"You know what Mother will say if you buy that picture?"

"That I've lost my taste?"

"That you never had any."

"I don't think I have to be entirely dependent on your mother's sometimes rather narrow puritanical ideals."

Still, she knew she had killed the purchase. Augusta's eye might have been almost too pure, her nose for sham too keen, but her veto would be final to a husband who had never openly admitted his festering suspicion that her taste was finer than his own.

"I've got to get back to the office," she muttered, ashamed of herself now. At the door she turned to smile ruefully at his adamantly presented back. He seemed to be appealing to the lady in pink to repudiate his daughter and her outrageous allegation. "If you insist on the mauve decade, why not try Boldini? Or Helleu? At least they were frankly fashionable."

Mark was away in Washington for a conference of museum directors, and she was alone that night. She took a sleeping pill to escape her mental agitation, and when she awakened at four in the morning it was with the total recall of a very vivid dream about Drew. She saw again his sullen brown eyes, his high-rising shiny black hair, and she uttered a groan at the return of her sensation of emotional captivity and frustration. For she had struggled so desperately to burrow behind the barrier of that critical stare, that rejecting disapproval of all her likes and dislikes, only to find herself in the prison camp of his nihilism. Oh, how she had yearned, pined, prayed, for some scrap of illusion, some rag of romanticism! But no. He had been consistently, remorselessly dry. She had had no conception that his politics were only the expression of his passionate resentment of his harsh, near fascist father and would be utterly transformed with maturity into a simpler form of social aggression. She had let him tear her past to shreds. He had turned a bleak light on her father, on her sisters, on her friends; he had fixed them in the same exposed circle in which he made his own family perform their silly dance.

"You know much better than I do, Julia, how many people and dollars it costs society to keep up your father's style of living. And what does he give in return? He buys pictures to donate them to a museum to lower his income and death taxes. If he didn't do this, others would. He is a perfectly useless person."

In her dream, however, it was not the memory of what he

had said of her father's collecting that had most upset her. It was the much sharper memory of her father's reaction to Drew and Drew's comment on *that.*

"You're making Daddy furious," she had protested. "Can't you ever shut up?"

"Not as furious as all that," the future investment banker had sneered. "He can always take a certain amount of criticism from a brawny young man."

And *that,* she knew in the anemic light of early morning, was what had released her from Drew at last. Not because *she* had not known about her father, but because *he* had. She had always been aware that Peter overtipped good-looking bellboys, that the new chauffeur was invariably handsome, that there were many more male nudes than female among his paintings and drawings and that he was beamingly charming to his daughters' more attractive beaux. She had even been amused by an anecdote he loved to tell of an eminent Victorian scholar, whose middle-aged maiden daughters, accompanying him on summer trips to Venice, had described his partiality for gondoliers as "Papa's little weakness." For she had always been sure that *her* papa's little weakness had never gone to such lengths. It had been a tamed, harmless thing, perhaps even contributing to his flair for art, and observed by only one person, in whose keeping it was perfectly safe.

But to have it perceived by Drew had been simply unbearable! She got up and tried to obliterate the memory with black coffee.

She spent a useless day at her office, too tired and upset to concentrate with much purpose on the new curtains for her Aunt Flora's dining room or the carpet for the lobby of 1116 Park Avenue. Quitting the office early, she went to her family's apartment, resolved to make up for her unkindness by pretending to her father that she had changed her mind about the Sargent.

After all, it was not *his* fault that she had made him the hero of her inward monodrama. It was no responsibility of his that she had woven the fantasy of the beautiful father-daughter relationship to shield her from anything in life that she had not deliberately picked out for herself, turning it this way and that to be sure it was just right for Julia Hewlett. It behooved her then, now that she had selected Mark, to be fair.

She was told that Mr. Claverack was with her father in his study. The latter had left word, however, that if she called, she was to join them there. Both men had been smoking, and the atmosphere was heavy. Passing her father to open a window, she noted with surprise how haggard he looked.

"Let me tell you at once, my dear, that Sidney has brought me some very bad news. I told you about the trouble over the appraisals. It now appears it was Mark who tipped off Uncle Sam."

She stared at the sallow-faced chairman as she took her seat. "Why would Mark do a thing like that? Out of good citizenship?"

"I have never known him to be so public-spirited," Sidney said sneeringly. "And wouldn't even the most conscientious citizen have given me the chance to explain the matter first? And even if my explanation had not satisfied him, wouldn't he have found some less drastic way of correcting the matter? Like asking me to file amended tax returns on the basis of later discovered error? But oh, no! The holy Mark has to smear me and smear my clients. And smear the poor old museum still covered with the smears of the ugly lawsuit caused by his seduction of the Vogel woman!"

"Please, Mr. Claverack! You are speaking of a friend of mine."

"No friend of yours, believe me, Julia. I am quite aware of your relations with him, but your father has authorized me to speak openly. Addams is a man who will stop at nothing to get his way. Because I have opposed him in his projects, he has planned to force my removal from the museum. If he happens to destroy me and my law practice at the same time, that's just the icing on the cake. And who will he replace me with? Who but the man whose compliance he has secured by the most adroit flattery in the world . . ."

"Too true, too true!"

Julia was shocked by the note of agony in her father's wail.

"And whose daughter," Sidney continued, with a savage smile, "he is counting on to bring him the fortune that every smart young museum director needs to carry him to the top of the social heap."

"Daddy, do you really believe all this?"

"But, my poor darling, I don't see that I have any alternative! How could Mark not have come to me first before going to the federal authorities? And when he did a thing like that, how can I look back to all the horror of that lawsuit and not see it in the very light I tried so hard *not* to see it in? Isn't it obvious now that Mark was trying to seduce that poor Vogel girl to gain control of the Speddon money? And when that backfired, and he knew Sidney was on to him, what did he do but turn to me and, through me, to *you*? In my naïveté I thought he was lonely, abandoned by his lawyer mistress. In fact, I see now that he probably kicked her out once she had won his suit and was no longer any use to him! The worst part of it all is that I've exposed you to this adventurer. Damn it all, Julia, I've actually thrust you into his arms!"

"Daddy, cool it, please. Nobody's thrust me into anyone's arms. I'm not a pillow."

She rose and walked to the books. Did she believe a word of it? Did she even care if it was true? She ran a fingernail over the bindings nearest her. The volumes that were turned face out to expose their golden armorial bearings were from the libraries of the maiden daughters of Louis XV. Red, green and yellow, with lozenges enclosing three lilies of France, they proclaimed their owners: Adelaide, Victoire, Sophie. As a girl she had wanted to write a book about them. Unmarried, living in the most beautiful palace in the world, surrounded by beautiful things, painted by Nattier — who said their lives were unfulfilled? Was her life unfulfilled? She turned back to the two men.

"Has Mark admitted that he went to the tax authorities?" she asked Claverack.

"On the contrary, he has denied it. But a Treasury official admitted to me that the tip came from the museum, and there is no one there but Addams who could have linked the appraisals to my office. In that, I have no doubt he enjoyed the assistance of his paramour."

"Do you refer to Chessie Norton?"

"That surprises you, doesn't it? You had thought their intrigue terminated? No, your father's wrong about that. When I voiced my suspicions to my new partner, for that is what, in my folly, I had made Miss Norton, she did not bother, like her confederate, to deny them. She simply informed me that she had just accepted a partnership in a newly organized all-woman law firm. What, you may ask, does she get out of all this? Perhaps Mr. Addams has promised her that he will buy her new firm a law library when he has wed his heiress."

"That strikes me, Mr. Claverack, as a contemptible suggestion. But not a bad idea. If Mark and I ever marry, that law library may be a joint gift."

"Julia, my child, you wouldn't marry him after this!"

"It's just what I might do, Daddy. If he's still willing to take the daughter of a man who let him down so cheaply."

And leaving the gaping pair, she walked out of the room with the lightest heart she had had in eight years.

16

"I'M SORRY, Miss Hewlett, I don't believe a word that you've told me."

Anita Vogel stared in cold anger across her desk at her handsome, importunate visitor. It seemed to her that this daughter of privilege was guilty of the ultimate insolence in invading her office to spray pellets of dirt over the character of Anita's one good friend. Was it not perversity in a princess to leave her palace to grab matches from the hand of the little match girl?

"You may be quite right, Miss Vogel. I only thought I had to tell you. I *know* Mark didn't do it."

"How can you know that?"

"Well, a woman can, you know. She can feel it."

"Then can't I feel the same about Dr. Sweeters?"

"Of course you can."

Like all princesses, she had to have the last word. She had to be reasonable, democratic, while her victim was making a fool of herself with ridiculous fantasies of being Hans Christian Andersen's match girl. Anita reflected bitterly that Miss Hewlett and her father were even worse than Claverack. The ex-chairman was simply a reptile; one knew that one had constantly to face him, never for a moment to turn one's back. But the Hewletts pretended to be men and women of good will; it was their confident conviction that they benefited the community. As they never doubted themselves, it did not occur to them that others could doubt them. Yet had Anita not seen Peter Hewlett endorse Claverack in the plotted wrecking of Miss Speddon's plans? Oh, *now* he was back on the side of the angels, sure, now that the battle had been fought to a temporary victory, now that it was fashionable once more to give lip service to "dear old Daisy's" ideals.

The princess had risen. "I hope you can forgive me, Miss Vogel. I thought I was doing my duty."

"If you were doing your duty, there's nothing to forgive."

"Good day, then, Miss Vogel."

Alone, Anita gazed miserably at the little red stone Mayan frog that Carol had given her on her birthday. They wanted to take even Carol from her now! She closed her eyes to sense the long sweep of the foaming remnant of a breaker up a flat beach. It reached her now, lying on the sand; she was half-inundated with pleasant water, and then it receded. Where would she be without his grumpiness, his nastiness, his odd way of showing a devotion that had survived her every coolness?

And there he was, frowning at her from the doorway.

"You know, I almost miss Claverack. There's no one left to hate around here."

"According to Miss Hewlett, who just left, you hate Mark."

"She came to tell you *that*?"

"Not in so many words. She thinks you were the one who broke the story of the appraisals."

"Not a bad guess."

She stared at him in horror. His grin had become fixed and . . . yes, *evil!*

"Carol, you didn't!"

"Oh, but I did, baby. That lawsuit didn't quite do the trick, did it? Claverack and Addams were only scotched. I had to give the poor fellows their *coup de grâce.*"

Her mind had become a furnace of Mayan tortures and a starved cat. "Oh, you can't have, you can't! You can't have been so vile."

"What the hell! You've been in this thing with me from the beginning. It was the only way to clean up this institution."

She leaned forward, her hands over her face. He moved around her to put an arm over her shoulders, but she shook him off. "Leave me be! I was right in the first place about the cat. I should never have forgiven you!"

She waited now for the angry screeching laugh that she remembered so vividly from their first real row. But it didn't come. And when she opened her eyes to look for him, he was gone.

She was ushered into the gallery, where the butler told her she was to wait for Mr. Hewlett. She spotted the El Greco at once and approached it gingerly. "When the Spaniards came to Mexico," Carol had told her once, "they found that even the Mayas had very little to teach them about cruelty."

But almost immediately she found herself studying the painting with the greatest intensity. It was a large, square canvas, full of billowing smoke over three stakes on which three writhing, elongated figures were chained, surrounded by a guard of gravely watching, golden-casqued soldiers. In the background was a view of a hillside Toledo, recalling the famous landscape at the Metropolitan. She noted that the expression on the faces of the soldiers, in contrast to the agonized, upward stares of the heretics, seemed composed. They were as calm and sober as the nobles in *The Burial of Count Orgaz.* She wondered whether their grim duty might have been an accepted routine, a ritual as automatic as a daily mass, and if the writhing of the victims was as much a part of the sacrament as the consecration of the bread and wine. What was, was, those pale faces seemed to be saying. Flesh blackened by fire and flesh encased in golden armor was the flesh of God, the flesh of the world.

"Do you find it significant that there are *three* stakes?" came a voice from behind her, and she turned quickly to face the collector.

"For the three crosses?"

"That's what usually strikes people. Though it would have been the most fearful heresy in that day. One can't assume that El Greco saw the heretics as martyrs. And yet it's hard for me to believe that he was on the side of those smug soldiers."

She found herself oddly at ease with his impromptu approach. "Maybe he sided with both. To a sensitive soul, wouldn't burning a man be as bad as being burned? Even worse?"

"To a *sensitive* soul, perhaps. But were Spanish soldiers sensitive? Was Cortez? Was Pizarro?"

"How do we really know? That may be just what the artist is trying to say. It might be a picture of the essential human condition. Torturing and being tortured."

"And all saved?"

"Or all damned."

"Dear me, Miss Vogel, what a dismal conclusion!"

"I don't know. At least they'd all be together!" It was certainly curious to be discussing such things with Mr. Hewlett. But she still had a sense of elation. Maybe what the painter was telling her was that she and Carol were one.

"Do you know there are actually people who think that painting wouldn't belong in the Museum of North America?"

"Really? I don't agree with them at all. You just mentioned Cortez. Can anyone deny the role that Spain, inquisitors as well as conquistadors, played in this continent?"

"But El Greco, they say, had nothing to do with all that. Of course, maybe he had nothing to do with the painting, either. Maybe it was done by some nineteenth-century Spanish artist."

"You mean it's a fake? Oh, Mr. Hewlett! Your masterpiece?"

"Stranger things have happened to collectors. But however interesting this subject is, I don't suppose it's what you came to discuss with me."

"In a way it may be. A friend of mine, I'm sorry to say, has done a very cruel thing. He thought he was justified, but there could be no justification. Any more than there was justification for *that.*" She pointed to the canvas. "I mean the burnings."

He looked at the painting as if considering this for the first time. "And was this cruel thing done to someone at the museum?"

She took in the twinkling condescension of his kindness. He was not taking her seriously. "To several persons, Mr. Hewlett. Including yourself."

"Me!"

"It was Carol Sweeters who told the Revenue people about the appraisals. He knew that you and Mr. Claverack would assume that Mark Addams had done it, and he wanted to get Mark into trouble. He has always hated Mark."

But Hewlett seemed abruptly indifferent to the motive. He actually clapped his hands.

"But this is wonderful news, Miss Vogel! You are quite right that the cruelty of the act redounded upon myself. For I make no secret of the fact that Mark and my daughter have been the closest friends. Perhaps you knew that?"

"It was she who suspected Carol."

"Indeed! Well, you can imagine how painful it was for me to think that Mark was undermining the institution of which he was director."

She turned to the door. "And now that that's been cleared up, I can go back to work."

Hewlett at this seemed to take in that there might be

repercussions in the matter even for one so lowly. "You're very kind to have come to tell me. Won't you stay and have a cup of tea or a drink? I can make it all right at the museum, if that's what you're worried about."

"No, thank you. I think I'd better go."

"But, my dear Miss Vogel, may this not have been distressing to you as well? You mentioned that Dr. Sweeters was a friend."

"Yes, and of course it's distressing when a friend behaves like that. And painful to have to tell on him. But I couldn't stand by and see Mark hurt."

"You saw that it *would* hurt him?"

"How could it not?"

"Mightn't a board of enlightened trustees take the attitude that he had simply done his duty as a citizen?"

"Would *you* think that, Mr. Hewlett?"

He sighed. "No, trustees are only human, and nobody likes a snitcher. But that gets me to my point. When I inform them, as I fear I must, of what you have just told me, will your friend Sweeters not be in just the hole that you have so generously pulled Mark out of?"

"But that will be his fault."

"I understand he has been offered an excellent position in California. Would he not be well advised to accept it?"

"Perhaps he will. When I tell him what I've done."

"Ah, you'll do that?"

"Do I have a choice?"

"You're a brave girl. But did I not hear that they want you, too?"

"Yes, but I wouldn't leave the museum so long as I could be of any help with the Speddon collection."

He smiled foxily. "You mean, so long as you're needed as a watchdog? Oh, even trustees know something of what goes on, Miss Vogel. But supposing I were to give you my word, as the new chairman of the board, that you will be kept informed of any proposed change in the disposition of Miss Speddon's things?"

She suddenly recalled her feeling at a children's party in Rye, given by her mother for her half-sister, when a smiling, insinuating, hand-fluttering gypsy of a trickman had somehow emptied her pockets without her feeling a thing and held up her miserable belongings to the laughing company. Were the Hewletts going to rob her of all her prejudices?

"Why would you undertake to do that?"

"Because I think we owe it to you. And because — let me be bold — I dare to speculate that you and Carol Sweeters, away from all this, may forget all about it."

"And live happily ever after?"

"That, my dear lady, is surely your affair and not mine."

His tone was a bit dryer; clearly, he was accustomed to having his big heart more readily appreciated. Well, what did she really have to gain from that turbid, windy organ?

"Let me ask you one thing, sir. Will Mr. Claverack be returning to the board?"

"A good question. The answer is no. Mr. Claverack is entering into a settlement with Uncle Sam, pursuant to which some heavy fines will be paid. And that will be the end of the matter. But the stipulations contain admissions on his part that will make it impossible, in my opinion, for the board to take him back."

"Thank you, Mr. Hewlett." There was no avoiding now what she had to say at the end. "And, really, you have been most kind."

It was her turn now to stand in the doorway. Carol did not look up from the paper he was pretending to read. But he obviously knew she was there.

"Can I help you, Miss Vogel?"

"I want to talk about the L.A. job. I thought I might take it, after all."

It was rare for Carol to let his expression admit surprise, but looking up now, he did so. "You mean you wouldn't mind working with a cat slaughterer?"

"Not if he promised never to do it again."

He rose. "What are you trying to tell me, Anita?"

"That we're in the same boat now."

"Going where?"

"To California. An hour ago you were in the position of having used confidential information to damage a friend of mine. Now things have changed. I'm just as guilty as you. I have told Mr. Hewlett what you did. I have restored Mark to his good graces and sent you to Coventry."

His face was like a field of battle before the first assault. He seemed to be waiting, prepared either for the bugle call of charge or the fluttering flag of truce.

"And you did that because Addams was such a dear friend?"

"I did it because I thought it was the right thing to do."

"And not just for him?"

"I'd have done it for anyone. I'd have done it for you, had things been the other way round."

"And how do you feel about the man who put you in the position of having to do it?"

"I've told you. We're in the same boat now. I feel about you exactly the way I feel about myself."

"Do you love yourself?"

"No."

"Not much!"

"I don't, Carol."

"Then you don't love me."

"Does that have to follow?"

"Then you *do* love me."

"Really, is this the place to discuss that? Can't you take me out to dinner tonight?"

"I suppose you've always loved me, really," he mused. "I've been an ass not to have seen it. Or did I really see it all along?

But yes, I'll take you out to dinner. Only tell me one thing. Don't you really think the less of me for what I did?"

"If it had been for the museum, as you said, I might have. But I think I liked your doing it out of jealousy."

He threw up his hands. "How remorselessly trivial can a woman be?"

She smiled as he stalked past her and out of his office. He was already counting the disadvantages of his new position, wondering if even a happy marriage would be worth her irrational sentimentality or the mother-in-law she would bring him. But then they would be starting a new life in California, far from all his and her old connections. It would probably be at least a year before he decided that he had left behind a better life in a better world. She shrugged, accepting now the prospect of his eternal discontent. It was the way he was.

17

PETER could never afterwards forget that the worst blow of his lifetime had come at the very moment he had thought his happiest. Augusta no doubt would have seen this as proof that he had never endured serious agony. But, then, Augusta had little sympathy for suffering that she deemed brought on by the sufferer.

It was at a dinner at the Oise, with Julia and Mark, to celebrate the reconciliation that had followed the revelations of Miss Vogel.

"Mark has something to tell you, Dad."

"I rather hoped you *both* had something to tell me."

"It's not what you think. That can wait."

"Not too long, I trust." He leaned over to wink at her. "At your age, my love, it's time for a girl to be thinking of her posterity."

"Really, Dad. I'm not an old woman yet."

"Of course not. But it's still time to get cracking."

"Mark has something to tell you about your new gallery. It's a decision that he and I have discussed and of which, I warn you, I highly approve."

Peter beamed at his prospective son-in-law. "Tell me, dear boy, what's on your mind." But he had his first premonition of disaster in the way that Mark straightened his features.

"Well, I guess you know, Peter, that I've had serious doubts from the beginning about your plan of juxtaposing European and American paintings in a museum devoted to one continent. Even as a means of demonstrating your theory of influences."

Peter, with death in his heart, swallowed hard. "Doubts? We all have doubts. There are few certainties in this vale of tears."

"I guess they're more than doubts, then. I don't deny that you have some fascinating and provocative theories. But in my opinion they're too speculative, too fanciful, if you will, to be so solidly implemented by a history museum."

"Which means?"

"Which means that I can't see my way to having a major part of our space dedicated to a project that is, first, only semi-related to North America, and secondly, of questionable validity."

"You can't see *your* way, you say? Why is your way suddenly so important?"

"Well, I *am* the director."

"Has the board not approved it?"

"Not officially, no. Of course, if you insist, I shall submit it to them. But at the same time I shall present my own arguments against it. That is what I had been hoping to avoid."

"Do you think for a moment, Mr. Addams —"

"Oh, Daddy, is it Mr. Addams now?"

"It certainly is. Do you think for a moment, sir, that the board would turn down the fabulous gift of my European paintings for *any* conditions that I might impose? From my knowledge of my co-fiduciaries, which is quite as good, I dare to presume, as yours, I should not deem them such killers of golden geese."

"If they should vote to accept your proposal, I should then put it to them that we ought to incorporate a separate museum: the Peter Hewlett Gallery of European Art."

"And if the board rejects that idea? If they agree to go ahead with my gallery and collection as planned?"

"Then I have no alternative but to resign."

"My God, man, are you mad?" Peter slapped his hand on the table so that the glasses tinkled. "Would you risk my giving my treasures to other institutions? What the hell sort of a director does that make you?"

"Daddy, let me introduce a note of calm. I think we could do with one. Mark has learned a lot of things since he came to the museum, and he's learned the hard way. He may have started out as the kind of young director you like to visualize: competitive, eager, even a bit tricky. Everything for my team, and to hell with the others. Like any hard-boiled corporate type. But now he has come to see — and he has made *me* see, too — the cultural world as a whole. And he and I both agree that it would be a better thing if your pictures were spread over the country rather than cooped up in one institution. And that, not even the appropriate one. And under an artificial common denominator, to boot."

"Which daughter of mine is speaking? Goneril or Regan?"

"Oh, Daddy. Must you be melodramatic?"

"Of course, we'd be happy to take the American pictures," Mark put in cautiously. "And place all of them in your special gallery."

"You'll take them my way or not at all!"

"Daddy, please don't have a temper tantrum."

"I'm not having a temper tantrum, Julia. I'm much too concerned for that. And I'm going home right now. You are welcome to finish your meal. Please order anything you want.

I'll tell Pierre to put it all on my bill, including the tip. Good night. I hope you have a charming evening discussing what an old idiot and philistine I am."

"Daddy!"

"If you'll just hear me out, Mr. Hewlett —"

"Good night!"

He found the apartment dark, with lights on only in the hall and the corridor leading to his bedroom. Augusta had retired. He went to the gallery and switched on the bulbs over each of the pictures so that they shone brilliantly and independently in the murky void. He walked slowly down the long chamber, pausing with an aching heart before every frame. Had ever a man been so treated by those he loved? Was the world worthy of his treasures? Stopping before the El Greco, he wondered whether it would not be a fitting end for him and his collection to expire like Sardanapalus in the conflagration of a giant funeral pyre.

"What happened tonight, Peter?"

Silhouetted in the hall light at the end of the gallery was the robed figure of Augusta.

"Addams doesn't want my things!" he cried out in a burst of agony. "He doesn't want my gallery. And Julia's put him up to it!"

"Oh, my poor darling." She came swiftly down the room and put her arms around him, pressing her head against his chest. "I thought this was coming. Never mind. There are lots of other things you can do with your paintings. Better things, too."

"No!" He broke away from her to resume his pacing. "That fellow is going to have the lesson of his life. We'll see whom the board will back: the young wise guy with the odor of the Speddon case still hanging about him or the old collector with a fortune to give away!"

"Sleep on it, Peter. We'll discuss it in the morning."

"I tell you, Augusta, I mean it! There isn't going to be any more talking. Except to my fellow trustees as to the disposition of Mr. Mark Addams."

"You can't mean it!"

"I never meant anything more."

"If you do that, Peter Hewlett, you will have become a monster."

"Augusta!"

"You will have allowed your crazy obsession with your gallery to eat up the last shred of your humanity. I'm afraid you will leave me no alternative but to take a very drastic step. So think before you leap, my dear. I am telling you now, in all sincerity, that if you do this thing to Mark *and* to Julia — for it will be as much to her as to him — I shall leave you."

And as if to illustrate the execution of her threat, she abandoned him to the morose examination of his pictures.

He knew, of course — he had always known — that she was the real founder of the collection. For it had been she, and not he, who had known how to handle his terrible father.

The elder Hewlett had always perversely sought to identify himself with the fiercest of the new rich of his day. On his graduation from Harvard, he had appalled his parents by going to work for the aging Jay Gould. He had progressed from railroads to oil to automobiles, and finally to the purer generality of the stock market, where the art of moneymaking was not hampered by a product, amassing a fortune which, if minor compared to those connected with the big names he so admired, was enough to give him respectable admittance to their league. Shelby Hewlett had affected the mien of the tycoon, with fur collars, gold chains, large cigars and coarse language, but he was always capable of shifting roles, if the case called for it, and putting one down with a cold stare, a sniff and a sneer like "No Yale man is ever quite a gentleman." For Shelby's joy was in playing the chameleon: the despot who brings a Scroogian turkey to an ill Cratchit child, the friend of Diamond Jim Brady who never missed a Sunday service in his front pew at St. George's, the self-proclaimed philistine who knew more about art than his morose, aesthetic only son.

Ah, but did he? Peter had a way of having the last word. It was all very well for his mother and sister, pallid females with haunted eyes, who expected and received the neglect of their lord, tempered only by a supercilious kindness, to put up with his stealthy exits and noisy returns, but Peter deemed himself made of sterner stuff. From childhood he had cultivated the virtues his father lacked. At St. Paul's School and at Harvard he had majored in the classic languages; he had scorned athletics and men's clubs; he had sought out the company of poets and artists and enjoyed the society of older women who kept salons. As a bachelor in the nineteen thirties he had started to collect, and filled a beautiful old house in Chelsea with paintings of the Ash Can School and sculptures of Lachaise and Brancusi. For his father had settled just enough capital on him at birth to make him independent, even rich, so long as he spent with a shrewd eye. The senior Hewlett came to regret his loss of control over his big, gangling, sarcastic heir, but there was a running competition between them in which both seemed to find stimulation. If Shelby, a small man, tried to puff himself up with tall heels to his black, ankle-high boots and with padded shoulders, Peter seemed to be minimizing his mass by a bent posture, a high voice and fluttering hands.

Peter's lip would curl as he passed under the portico of his father's baroque mansion on Madison Avenue and faced the eclectic clutter of French eighteenth-century furnishings, "improved" by the heavy hand of a Victorian decorator.

"Heavens! Something new again. Will there be no end to your magnificence, sir? Who did that incomparable *fête champêtre?*"

"Lancret."

"But, my worshipful sire, that little painting isn't even *trying* to be a Lancret."

"Of course, it wouldn't suit an Ash Canner unless one of the huntsmen were taking a pee."

"Do you know, that's precisely what it needs? You *do* have an eye!"

There was a theory among their acquaintance that father and son really loved each other, but Peter knew that was not true. His father was too much an egoist to love anyone, and Peter at times wondered somberly if that was going to be true of himself. But Augusta, a mere twenty when he was thirty-four, convinced him at last that his case was not hopeless. Everyone had marveled at her choice. Beautiful, popular, and well enough off to be beyond the suspicion of seeking the fortune that an eccentric millionaire might well leave away from his impertinent son, she had somehow found in Peter what she wanted. Perhaps it was simply that she fancied she saw what she might do with him. He only needed, perhaps, a little adroit straightening out to take his proper place in society as an *arbiter elegantiarum*, a stalwart family man and even a sufficiently important citizen. And indeed, as the years passed, Peter would stiffen in posture, expand in girth, begin to speak in deeper tones, as if the butterfly of the gaudy tycoon were emerging from the chrysalis of the pale aesthete. Was *that* what she had wanted? But then one never quite knew what Augusta wanted.

She started by coming to frank terms with her father-in-law.

"Everyone agrees that you're a great businessman, Mr. H, but you're going to have to prove it to me. My father's a pretty good businessman himself, and he's always told me a good trader never wastes a capital asset. It seems to me you're doing just that with Peter."

"Is this a way of telling me, my pretty one, that I should shovel more gold down the drain of that decorous idler?"

"He's idle only from lack of resources. Peter has a fantastic flair for art. I know you don't share his taste, but as a good investor you should be able to spot its potential. Did you actually want to drive that terrible car — what was it called? — that you put so much money into? Of course not. You simply saw it would sell. I don't think I underrate you when I say that you *know* that Peter has a better eye than you do. Put money in it then. I'm not asking it for myself or for living expenses. Give it to Peter to buy pictures. You'll never regret it. Let me put it more strongly. It will make your name remembered when everything in this house is forgotten."

Shelby Hewlett winced. "You do put it on the line, my girl. I won't say I like it. But you're right about not wasting principal assets. I'm not going to waste *you.*"

Compliments were lost on Augusta. "So long as you do it."

And so Peter's major collection had begun. His father ultimately even took pleasure in it, particularly when it spread to a showy royal portrait by Van Dyke or a lovely lady with powdered hair by Romney, though he was always disappointed at how briefly his son lingered in such fields.

Things changed, however, after Peter's mother died. That self-effacing lady must have exercised more control than she had been given credit for, for her widower rapidly sank into coarse and erratic ways. When he began to drink heavily and womanize, few respectable members of society cared to cross his threshold. Peter himself would not have him in the house because he upset the girls, and only Augusta's firmness prevented a total breach. When Shelby married a tough redhead, forty years his junior, Peter's maiden sister fled to an apartment hotel, and even Augusta ceased calling at the baroque mansion.

The will, when Shelby's disorderly life came to its disorderly close, was not a surprise. After provision of a trust fund for the maiden daughter, the residuary estate was divided: one-third to Peter and two-thirds to the widow.

Peter had no wish to contest. He pointed out to Augusta that his father, despite obvious eccentricities, had been of sound mind.

"He knew what he was doing. He wanted not so much to enrich Lola as to humiliate me. The only reason I got a third was to show the world that he cared for his whore exactly twice as much as he cared for his son. Also, perhaps, to keep me from suing."

"We'll see who has the last laugh," Augusta retorted. "For of course you're going to sue."

"Even if I can't prove undue influence?"

"But you can."

"Do you honestly believe, Augusta, that my father was so much under the influence of that woman as not to know the natural objects of his testamentary bounty? For that's the legal test, you know. I've already discussed it with counsel."

"So have I. And with the same counsel, John Whinney, after you had finished with him. He quite agreed with me. The question is not what the law is, but how it will be applied in a particular case. A judge and jury are perfectly capable of understanding and applying the moral law that underlies the common law. Maybe a man in his right mind can strip his family for an ex-prostitute, but a court may find it conclusive evidence of a very wrong one."

"And say so? In those words?"

"A court doesn't have to give all its reasons. You had better let John Whinney make these decisions. Otherwise you will be taking on your own shoulders the responsibility of throwing in the gutter money that might purchase and preserve for posterity some of the most beautiful things in the world."

Peter bowed to her opinion, and a long scandalous lawsuit ensued in the Surrogate's Court of the County of New York. Mr. Whinney proved himself adept at digging up mountains of dirt in the past of Lola Hewlett, to the delight of readers of the evening journals, and at driving it through rules of evidence like a garbage truck through willow fences. When Peter protested to his wife that Lola's past was not relevant to the issue of testamentary capacity, she simply responded, "Is our evidence true or isn't it?"

"Oh, I daresay it's true enough."

"Then that should be good enough for us. I don't say I mightn't agree with you if John Whinney were smearing the woman with lies. But he's not."

There was little question but that the public agreed with Augusta and that the court seemed likely to. Before the plaintiff had rested his case, Mrs. Hewlett's counsel sought a settlement, and their client ultimately accepted a reduction of her share of the residuary estate from two-thirds to one-tenth. It was a signal victory, and everyone agreed that Whinney had earned his fee of a quarter of a million dollars.

Peter was now able to collect to his heart's content, but, oddly enough, with increased revenues, Augusta seemed to take less interest in his acquisitions. At first he thought that she missed the excitement of hunting big game with a limited supply of bullets, but a deeper reason appeared in her lack of sympathy with his use of categories to give form and meaning to his collecting. She could never see why he should tie himself down to a particular century or nation, and she had no patience with the classifying of art into portraits or landscapes or still lifes or even abstracts. But what annoyed her most of all was his buying with an idea of furnishing some future gallery in a museum.

"Why don't you just *look*?" she would say. "Look and buy. So long as it's beautiful, so long as it speaks to you, why do you care when it was painted or by whom? Or even of what?"

He could never tie her down to a "favorite" painting or paintings, or even to a much preferred one. Augusta was nothing if not eclectic. She would subside into silent reverie before a Chinese scroll painting or a Byzantine reliquary or a Jackson Pollock or an Arshile Gorky. She avoided the jargon of critical language and seemed to have no desire to talk or even read about art. Peter speculated that she might have adopted Walter Pater's theory of the viewer as an essential complement to a work of art, completing it differently in different generations, and that the marriage of the creator and his audience was itself the artifact without need of expressed comment.

A simpler interpretation might have been that it was part and parcel of Augusta's increasing detachment from life as she grew older. Certainly the girls noted it, and were often hurt by the cool impartiality with which she regarded their personal problems. When Inez's husband deserted her, to the outrage of her father and sisters, Augusta refused to join in the clamor of denunciation, and was heard to make dry comments about what modern husbands had to put up with. And when Peter had decried the radicalism of Julia's socialist lover, she had simply remarked that the young man must have seen enough in their milieu to wish to visualize a new and braver world. But there had been one terrible moment, for which Peter wondered if he would ever find it in his heart to forgive her, when she had forsaken her usual habit of distancing herself from the fray to burst out, as he was holding forth to the girls at a family dinner about his theories of influencing: "Oh, Peter, I'm so sick of all that! Why must you go on with it? Why must you scribble 'Peter Hewlett' all over the wonderful things you've bought? You're like a little boy chalking 'Jack loves Lucy' on the side of some noble monument. Can't you leave your masterpieces alone? Do you think they can't speak for themselves?"

Sitting alone now in the dark room under the lighted glory of the pictures, Peter reflected that she always meant what she said. And now she would certainly leave him if he did what he threatened. It was even possible that she would never return. What was impossible was that he should let her go. He had lived too long in the presence of her disapprovals to contemplate with any complacency what his life would be in their absence. At least while she was with him he could exercise some containment of her criticisms. Away from him, who could tell what their boundaries might be?

Almost irately he rose now to turn off all the lights by the master switch. Very well! Did that satisfy her? There he was, Peter Hewlett, a nothing in the blackness of the void that only his money had been able to illuminate. The sole light now was in the doorway where he had seen Augusta's robed figure. He saw it again, in his mind's eye, this time no longer as a high priestess, but as an aging woman, her gray hair in curlers (oh, yes, even Augusta had her little vanities!), a puffy wrapper enveloping the bony shape so cleverly enhanced by her gowns. Why was she so somber? Was she jealous of the collection, of Julia, of Mark?

He could bear the darkness no longer. He illuminated the El Greco. Could there not be more than one truth and one Peter Hewlett? Did he *have* to see himself as an old fool, half-crazed by anger at the handsome young man he had wanted as a protégé?

Oh, there were moments, there were times . . . There were always moments and times. Had he not once wanted to kill his own father? Had there not been a day when Inez, as a chubby, shameless youngster, had aroused feelings of lust in him? Had he not actually hoped, when Augusta had that cancer scare, that she would die? Which were the martyrs in the auto-da-fé, the writhing heretics, condemned to a quick demise, or the placidly watching soldiers, condemned to a long one?

Looking up, he thought for a moment that Augusta had come back and was standing again in the doorway. But no, it was still empty. Now he imagined that he saw her again, without the curlers or the puffy wrapper, once more a priestess, a goddess from the machine. The embodiment of what? His conscience? He grasped at the notion; he seemed to snatch at it, as if to quell the rising rustle of sneers in the darkness, mocking his twaddle. Well, why *not?*, he retorted to the whispers. Might not imagined absolution be as real as imagined guilt? Maybe it was only horse sense to do as Augusta bade.

One by one now he turned on all the picture lights again and repaced the gallery slowly. There was, after all, a way of facing facts if he chose. With self-discipline he could dredge them up from the sludge of his illusions and self-pity. It might even prove a kind of anesthetic. Facts were not supposed to be pain-killers, but could they not be, if the self-deception had been lurid enough?

Very well. Here was one fact. Every painting in that room was a great one. Here was another. Augusta had chosen the best. She had even chosen the El Greco, which was probably a fake. But she had chosen it not because it was an El Greco: she had chosen it because it was great. More facts. His eye was good, but not as good as hers. And as to his theories of the development of American painting, did they not range from the obvious to the fanciful? That slick volume, showily illustrated from his own collection, that he had written and privately published to expound them, what had it been but an effort to conceal the inadequate critic behind the glorious accumulator? He had even hoped, had he not, by exposing his eccentric, cantankerous but supposedly lovable personality, to persuade the purchasers of that expensive tome that he was himself a kind of artist?

Other facts? Did they matter? He cared for Julia and Mark, but not really importantly. He had probably come as close to love with Augusta as he had ever come to that emotion. Was it another fact that he was facing all this?

Enough! He would put off the many-colored robe of his masterpieces, and when he had done so, he would be as bony as Augusta but with a pot beside, a naked old man whom she, for arcane reasons of her own, had seemed to love.

. . .

He sat up all night in his study, making lists. The collection would be disposed of, part in his lifetime, the rest on his death. The American paintings would be given to the Museum of North America. Of the European masters, one-third would be sold at auction and the proceeds placed in trust for the girls. Another third would be donated to museums across the country, in accordance with their needs and fitness. The final third would be retained for his lifetime and would pass under his will, half to the Museum of North America and half to his family. Except that the museum would have the right to dispose of its share by sale or otherwise, as it elected.

In the dull light of dawn he reduced his plan to a neat memorandum in purple ink. He then slipped it under Augusta's door and retired to his own room. He slept a dreamless sleep and awoke at noon, rested, sullen and resigned.

He found Augusta in the dining room. She must have been waiting for him for hours.

"You're a great man," she said quietly. "I always knew there was a great man in you somewhere. I suppose it's why I married you."

"You've had a long wait."

"It was worth it."

"Oh, Augusta, I'm so wretched!"

"My poor darling. That will pass."

There was a letter on his place from Carol Sweeters. It announced his resignation from the museum staff and thanked Peter for his hint to Miss Vogel that the time had come to take the California job. He concluded with a postcript that a recent test had proved the vision serpent a fake.

Peter uttered a high cackle of laughter as he handed the letter to Augusta. "He says he still believes in it. Do you know what I'll do? When it's been deaccessioned I'll buy it and send it to him as a wedding present."

"Is he going to marry that girl?"

"I think so. Anyway, that might clinch his purpose."

"Julia called this morning. I told her all was forgiven. She and Mark have set a date. Next month."

"Really!"

"And I told them what your wedding present would be. A spanking trust fund. I don't know if I really approve of that, but Julia has always been sensible about money."

"You told them so that I couldn't change my mind!"

"No, I trust you, my darling. Only it never hurts to add a little guaranty."

"Do you think they'll be happy?"

"Oh, yes. Mark, with everything he wants, will lose a bit of his shine. He may even become a tiny bit dull. But he will be good-tempered and conscientious, and he will do a fine job at the museum. Not that I care so much about that."

"And Julia?"

"Oh, she'll have several children and become very domestic. One has seen that before with cool professional women."

"Will she give up her career?"

"It depends on what you call her career. No woman ever gives up decorating. But her real career will be running the museum, for which she is even more qualified than he. It amuses me to think that Mark probably imagines, in kicking free from you, that he'll be independent of the Hewletts. But now he'll be controlled by the right one. And that will be all for his good."

Peter, drinking his coffee, black as he always liked it, reflected that in dismantling his collection he was only dismantling his presumptions. There could not be any great satisfaction in becoming nothing, but neither could there be much in pretending one was anything else. If the gods were all around one, maybe the best one could do was to be a vision serpent and hallucinate that one was, after all, a god too.